THE FRiENDSHiP BRACELET

THE FRIENDSHIP BRACELET

Arlene Stewart

sourcebooks
jabberwocky

Published by Sourcebooks Jabberwocky, an imprint of Sourcebooks, Inc.
P.O. Box 4410, Naperville, Illinois 60567-4410
(630) 961-3900
Fax: (630) 961-2168
www.sourcebooks.com

Library of Congress Cataloging-in-Publication data is on file with the publisher.

Source of Production: Versa Press, East Peoria, Illinois, USA
Date of Production: May 2017
Run Number: 5009404

Printed and bound in the United States of America.
VP 10 9 8 7 6 5 4 3 2 1

For Lee and Jana, my two funny Katonah girls.

Love you both!

CHAPTER 1

"Paris!" exclaimed Olivia Jones. "You're moving to Paris!"

Boom! Her entire summer went up in flames.

Worse: her whole life fell apart.

Because without Alex—without popular, funny Alex LeBrun—how was Olivia ever going to survive the ordeal of middle school? The tallest-shyest-klutziest-kid-in-sixth-grade ordeal?

Suddenly, Olivia's long, thin legs felt wobbly, and she slumped down on her bed like a newborn colt, her face totally colorless, her hands shaking. Sensing her distress, Sullivan, her two-year-old golden retriever, leaped up beside her.

Alex looked down at Olivia and felt helpless. She knew Olivia's reaction would be bad, but she hadn't thought it would be this bad. "Please, please, Ollie, please don't go crazy," she pleaded over and over.

Olivia was unable to do anything but sit still. She couldn't believe that *up until a minute ago* she had actually thought this was going to be a great day. Who doesn't love the first day of summer vacation?

But now, instead of her days being filled with fun, her heart was filled with a dread she had never known before. Tears rolled down her flushed cheeks and strands of her long, blond hair stuck to her face.

"Oh, Ollie, don't *cry!*" said Alex, pushing in beside Sullivan. "Maman made us promise not to tell anyone until Papa's transfer was official. Keeping this from you was the hardest thing I've ever had to do. Honestly!"

Alex rubbed her friend's back and looked around Olivia's light-blue bedroom. Dozens of photos illustrated their inseparable-BFF story: every birthday, every Christmas, every Fourth of July, every Halloween since the first day of preschool to last night's moving-up ceremony from Village Elementary, when Alex won the math prize and Olivia the English.

Her gaze fell on Olivia's desk, and that was when she almost lost it. The two identical purple-and-white friendship bracelets they'd been making for each other were laying there side by side…unfinished.

"When do you have to go?" Olivia finally asked, her lip quivering.

"In a couple of weeks," Alex replied. "Papa's office has arranged *un appartement* for us while we look for something permanent."

"Permanent!" cried Olivia, her worst fears confirmed. Alex was moving from New York to Paris—only three thousand miles away or more!

Fresh tears flowed down her cheeks and fell onto her Camp Monroe T-shirt, one from last summer. It felt so tight now. Why hadn't she realized it wouldn't fit? She had grown six inches in the past year! Maybe she really was a giraffe or one of the other horrible names creepy Ethan Fleckman kept calling her.

There was a gentle knock at the door. Olivia's mother slowly opened it and looked in at the sad scene.

"Oh, Mom, it's all right," said Olivia, wiping her face

on the shirt. "Alex just told me their family is moving to Paris in two weeks. That's all."

"Yes, Ollie, I know," said her mother softly. "Alex's mother already called me."

"What? Everybody knew but me?" cried Olivia, feeling like a total freak. "I've got to get out of here!" She jumped up, brushed past her mother, and thundered down the staircase with Sullivan fast at her heels.

"Where are you going?" shouted her mother over the bannister.

"I don't know. Anywhere. To Katonah Cupcakes!"

"Wait for me!" cried Alex, grabbing their shoulder bags.

CHAPTER 2

"It's Always Time for a Cupcake—Open Saturdays at 10:00" said the hand-lettered sign propped on a cake plate in the storefront of Katonah Cupcakes.

Olivia peered inside. A big clock by the register said 9:15. It was way too early, but before they could even think about someplace else to go, Alex's phone rang.

"It's my mother. I have to take it," she said to Olivia. "*Oui, Maman?*" she answered. Holding her hand over the phone, she explained in a whisper, "Maman is making us speak French all the time now. *Oui, Maman?*"

Olivia nodded. Over the years, she'd picked up a lot of French from Alex's family.

"I have to go home and help Maman figure out what

to take with us and what to donate to the hospital thrift shop," Alex said, hanging up. "Come over later?"

Olivia hesitated.

"Come on, Ollie. We have to find a way to make it better!" Alex insisted.

"OK. I'll text you."

"Got to go. Bye," said Alex, hurrying away.

Rigid as a stop sign, Olivia stood on the street corner, watching her BFF disappear down the block.

"*Beep, beep!* Out of the way, Beanpole!" Ethan Fleckman's booming voice startled her.

She twisted around and jumped out of the way of his flying skateboard. "Ethan, you almost ran into me!" she cried.

"Nah. I was totally in control," replied the sturdy boy with the thick, black hair and dark eyes that Olivia always imagined had come from some distant Asian ancestor. She couldn't help checking out his outfit. Wasn't there something weird about wearing a New York Rangers practice shirt and helmet with flip-flops?

"Hey, what time does your mother's shop open?" he said. "I need my new threads, Beanie."

Maybe I should call him some names too, Olivia thought. *I could think of some good ones…* But instead she said, "Ten o'clock, *as usual*." Her mom taught her to always be polite to Katonah Crafts customers, even exasperating ones like Ethan, a major friendship-bracelet guru who practically lived there.

"Cool," replied Ethan. "So where's your Siamese twin?"

"If you mean Alex…she's home."

"Cool." Ethan laughed and coasted off.

Olivia shook her head, crossed Bedford Road to the Parkway, and walked slowly down the block to her house. Like most of the houses in the village, it was a big, old-fashioned Victorian built well over one hundred years ago with a wide, wraparound front porch, shutters, and lots of bay windows.

Olivia's mom was in the front garden picking roses. "What happened?" she asked.

"Nothing!" muttered Olivia as she walked up the steps

and flung open the front door. "I'm going to my room. I need to be alone."

"Well, take Sullivan with you," her mother called after her and then cut off a big thorn on a beautiful yellow rose.

CHAPTER 3

"Call Me Maybe" woke Olivia at seven the next morning. It was Alex. "I'm on packing duty, and Maman is cracking the whip until we're done," she said breathlessly. "But listen, Ollie, Papa wants to teach us how to Skype. Your dad said OK. Can you come over at eleven?"

After a noticeable pause Olivia asked, "Will your papa be teaching us in French—*en français*?"

"Very funny," Alex replied. "Come on, Ollie."

"OK…"

"Good!"

"Don't you mean *d'accord*?" said Olivia, clicking off. She reached under the bed for her slippers, getting them on her feet a second before Sullivan tried to steal them.

"Oh, was that Alex?" asked her mother, walking by with a coffee mug.

"Yes," replied Olivia.

"And?"

"And I'm going over there at eleven."

"You are? That's wonderful, sweetheart," said her mother.

Olivia stood up. "Um," she said, dashing out of the room, "I'm going to take a shower."

"Use ours. I just got some new shampoo," shouted her mom.

In the bathroom, a note was taped on the mirror. "Look in my dresser—there's a surprise for you. XXXOOO, Mom." *Guess Mom knew I was headed this way*, thought Olivia.

As she stepped into the shower, a calmness poured over her like a silky coating of bodywash. The sharp needles of water felt extra-invigorating, and her mom's new shampoo wasn't bad either. Revived, Olivia dried off and remembered the note: "Look in my dresser."

She pretty much knew everything her mother owned.

She had realized at a young age that complete access to all your parents' things was one of the perks of being an only child.

Pulling out the top three drawers, she quickly discovered nothing unusual. Before she could reach the bottom drawer, Sullivan came prancing in with her old tennis shoe in his mouth.

"Hey, give that to me." Olivia laughed, wrestling away the shoe. She leaned over to open the last drawer.

Right on top was a gift bag with a card that said "Ollie." *What is this?* She reached for it. It was way too light for a new phone, although that would have been cool. Still puzzled, she plowed through a mound of tissue paper.

"Ooh," she said, taking out a pair of black, patterned tights. They were the ones she had seen at the mall…the ones her mom thought were too "mature" for her. *Guess Mom got them yesterday—to make me feel better*, Olivia quickly realized.

Spotting a pencil on top of the dresser, Olivia scribbled "Thanks! Love you!" on the note and then added a heart.

Without warning, Sullivan started to bark. Right

away, Olivia realized what he wanted—the tissue paper. It was his true passion. Sheet by sheet, Olivia threw the paper high in the air and watched as he jumped to snag each one. *This never gets old*, she thought with a smile.

With Sullivan happily shredding, Olivia leaned down to close the drawer but then noticed something unfamiliar—what looked to be a small leather pouch tucked in a back corner. When she picked it up, she could see that the leather was faded and cracked.

"Where did this come from, Sully?" she asked in a puzzled voice, plopping on her parents' bed. "Jeez, this knot is so tight."

Finally, she said with satisfaction, pulling the bag open, "There!"

Coiled inside was a well-worn friendship bracelet in shades of sky blue and white. Olivia examined the arrow pattern, a fairly simple one she had used a lot when her mom was teaching her the basics.

"We're home!" Olivia's dad boomed from downstairs.

Sullivan jumped from the bed and raced out with bits of tissue paper hanging from his mouth.

Better put this back, thought Olivia, slipping the pouch into the dresser drawer. Straightening up, she asked herself, *Was I supposed to find this? How come I've never seen it until now?* Before anyone could come looking for her, she grabbed her new tights and ran back to her room.

At first she reached for her cutoffs and tank top but then stopped. *No, I'm not going to dress like old Olivia*, she decided. Instead, she pulled out her best shorts and a brand-new Alexander Hamilton Middle School T-shirt in white and purple, her new school colors.

Then, standing before her mirror, she brushed her long hair up into a ponytail. *I'm not going to be nothing*, she told her image. *I don't care how tall I get—or what Ethan Fleckman thinks.*

CHAPTER 4

The next morning started with breakfast burritos, one dish Olivia's dad totally crushed.

"Seriously yummy, Dad," she said, trying to get her plate into the dishwasher without Sullivan licking it. "Stop, Sullivan, I have to go." In her haste, she stepped into his water bowl. Great—now her tennis sneakers were soaked.

"I'll wipe it up. You just go," said Olivia's dad, shooting her a thumbs-up as she headed to the mudroom for her bike helmet and tennis racquet. Lessons started at nine o'clock, and Olivia liked to be early.

As she pedaled up to the town park, a light mist covering the hilltop reminded her of an old nursery rhyme: "One misty, moisty morning, when cloudy was the weather, I chanced to meet an old man clothed all in leather." But as she approached the courts, the mist lifted and she could see a few teenage girls but no old men. Most were texting, but then she noticed a couple who were weaving friendship bracelets fastened with safety pins to their cutoffs.

That reminds me, she thought, *I have to follow up on that mysterious friendship bracelet in Mom's drawer. And maybe I have time to make a special going-away one for Alex. One in pink, her favorite color.*

"Hey, Olivia!" a cheerful voice interrupted her thoughts.

She looked over to see Mu Mu Lin, a girl she had bumped into every now and then at Alex's house, when Mu Mu was taking French lessons from her BFF's mother.

"Bummer about Alex's family moving away," Mu Mu said, brushing back her long, straight, black hair. "Mom is making me go to a new French tutor, tout de suite, although she keeps saying there's nobody like Madame LeBrun."

"Oh, hi, Mu Mu," replied Olivia. "Are you here for the tennis lesson?"

"I wish. My dopey brother left his phone on the court yesterday. Can you believe it? I have to go to the office and pick it up. Mom's in the car. Gotta go before she freaks out—again! See you in camp?"

"Town camp? Great," said Olivia, waving good-bye. Mu Mu had graduated from Meadowlark Elementary, a different school than Village Elementary, but this fall, they'd both be in Alexander Hamilton Middle School. *Well, at least I have one friendly person in my new class*, she thought.

Ten minutes later, a whistle blew.

"Advanced beginners, line up!" yelled Mr. Ocampo, the summer athletics director.

Olivia walked over to the court and was puzzled that the older girls she'd seen earlier were actually in her group. Then, the instructor trotted onto the court—a tall, good-looking teenager with Prince Harry–red hair and freckles. *Mystery solved*, thought Olivia, laughing to herself.

"This is Tatum Donnelly, and he'll be your instructor," announced Mr. Ocampo, checking off names on a clipboard.

"Can you believe he's only a junior?" one excited girl whispered to a friend behind Olivia.

After thirty minutes of serving and volleying with the older girls, Olivia was feeling pumped. She had more than held her own against them. Tatum blew his whistle and called the group together at the net.

"So, Olivia, you already have a strong serve. How old are you again? Fifteen?" he asked.

Fifteen! Olivia thought she'd seriously fry under the harsh glare from his fan club. She just smiled—she wasn't going to say she was eleven in front of this crew.

After the first game, Tatum paired her with a tallish boy Olivia had never seen before.

The first thing she noticed, besides his height, was the adorable way his sun-bleached curls framed his tanned face. He seemed to be about her age and was wearing baggy, white cargo shorts and a tank top that said "Endless Summer."

"Surfer Dude" she instantly named him in her mind.

As he chased her serves, his body moved well, and he even smiled at her when she scored against him.

Toward the end of their game, she felt overheated and called time. She shook out her ponytail for a few seconds and then gathered her long hair and put it up again. When she lifted her racket, she was surprised to see Surfer Dude staring at her.

But before she could catch his name, he was rotated off, and Hannah Bojarski, a girl she knew from flute lessons, took his place.

When the lesson ended at eleven, Olivia casually scanned the courts and then the park for him. *Blast!* He was nowhere to be seen. Practically everyone had gone home or to lunch. *Guess I better go too*, she thought, putting on her blue helmet. *Wonder if Surfer Dude will be here again tomorrow…*

CHAPTER 5

"Au revoir! Au revoir!"

Alex was hanging out of the back window of the limousine, waving good-bye. All too soon, the day had arrived for the LeBrun family to catch their flight.

"Au revoir! Au revoir!" shouted Olivia. As the limo pulled out of the driveway, she caught her reflection shining on its side and windows, and a poetic vision floated before her—maybe her image would fly along with them. But a moment later, the limo turned onto Bedford Road and her image vanished along with Alex.

Well, she told herself, the moment she dreaded had finally arrived and she was still breathing.

She straightened her shoulders and walked over to Main Street. Four shops in from the corner was Katonah

Crafts, her mom's store, with its barrels of white Shasta daisies outside by the roomy front stoop.

As she opened the door, a bell rang, and once more, Olivia was reminded how much she loved every inch of the old-fashioned shop. She loved that her mom kept the original high tin ceilings, lazy fans, wooden floors, and the built-in shelves, which used to seem so tall to her. Her mother made sure to stock skeins of yarn and embroidery flosses in every neon, pastel, and regular color imaginable along with tons of weaving materials: string, hemp, silky cord, pearl cotton, and more.

Summer was the busiest season, and this afternoon, Katonah Crafts was humming with young boys and girls checking out the beads, crafts books, scrap papers, and friendship bracelet supplies. Even the sight of Ethan Fleckman standing over by the cash register couldn't lessen the pleasure Olivia took in her mother's shop.

That is until the sound of high-pitched giggling burst the spell. Over by the jewelry supplies, a group of her old fifth grade Village Elementary classmates were laughing and texting. She made eye contact and waved hello.

Nobody waved back.

That's weird, Olivia thought, feeling dumped on. *A total diss? Is this a preview of middle school? Oh no!* Thoughts swirled through her head: *Maybe they didn't say hello because they didn't see me? Maybe because they're busy texting? Or maybe because at the center of the group, like a major star in a constellation, is Elin Pierson, only the most popular girl since forever?*

But was that really Elin? Olivia had to look twice—Elin's light-blond hair seemed to have grown more than a foot since school let out last week. Maybe that happened because her mother owned Magic Tresses, the hair styling salon Elin always let everybody know about. Could Elin's magic tresses actually be extensions?

Looking around to locate her own mother, Olivia noticed one of Elin's squad, Kennedy Washington, whispering something to Elin.

"Who?" asked Elin in a loud, peevish voice.

Kennedy pointed to Olivia.

Instantly, Elin turned on a smile and strolled over.

"Hi, Livia," she said, taking off her leopard-print sunglasses. "This is your mother's store? It's so awesome!"

"Oh, thanks, Elin," said Olivia.

"Yeah, it's stellar," chimed in her friends.

"Do you ever give out free samples?" purred Elin. "Like my mother does at Magic Tresses?"

Yuck! Olivia felt as trapped as a pelican in an oil slick. Desperately, she looked for help and saw Miss Ruth Ann, her mother's invaluable store manager, heading toward them. *Whew...*

Trying to get out of the way, Olivia stepped backward and bumped smack into a table display piled high with birdhouse kits. *Crash!* Several hit the old wooden floor, making a loud noise.

Ethan Fleckman glanced up from his flosses catalog and shook his head. Elin and her friends started giggling. Olivia could hear one of them muttering, "Klutz!"

Miss Ruth Ann ignored the disturbance. Instead, she said in a firm voice, "Good afternoon, girls. How may we help you?" She looked at them over her wire-framed glasses. A retired school secretary with dark skin and frizzy gray hair, Miss Ruth Ann was so no-nonsense that even Olivia's father, the by-the-book head of Katonah's Building Department, made sure to be on his very best behavior around her. Naturally, Olivia's mom loved her.

Olivia leaned down to pick up the birdhouse kits. Straightening up, she caught her mother's eye and signaled toward the entrance. Nearing the door, she could hear Miss Ruth Ann asking Elin, "And what is your budget, young lady?"

Two minutes later, her mother emerged. "Have a good night, dear," she said to Miss Ruth Ann with a wave. "See you in the morning."

Olivia's mom led her down the shop-lined streets toward their car. "Was that Pippi Pierson's daughter? With the sunglasses?" she asked. "Maybe you would like to spend some time with her this summer?"

Olivia rolled her eyes.

"Well, maybe not," her mom said. "Any thoughts about where to have dinner?"

Olivia's father was away on a two-day municipal

building conference, so Olivia and her mother got to be bachelorettes and eat out.

"Can we go to Golden Panda for takeout?" Olivia asked.

"You're not saying that just so you can give Sullivan the fortune cookies, are you?" her mother teased.

"No, Mom. But he does have his eye on my new black tights," said Olivia. "I can't wait to wear them. But maybe I should save them for school?"

"Then promise you won't grow over the summer," replied her mom with a laugh.

CHAPTER 6

"And can we please get lots of extra duck sauce?" a young girl was asking.

Mu Mu Lin was in front of Golden Panda's pickup counter when Olivia and her mother entered the bright-red-and-gold restaurant.

Standing near her, an Asian woman was texting on a cell phone. *That's probably Mu Mu's mother*, thought Olivia. They looked a lot alike, with small, pretty features and slender builds, only Mu Mu's mother was wearing a dark business suit and heels, and Mu Mu was dressed in a bright-yellow tank top and cutoffs.

"Hey, Olivia!" shouted out Mu Mu. "You eat here too? Don't they have absolutely the best spring rolls?"

"Hi, Mu Mu," Olivia replied in a much quieter voice. "Yup, and I love their General Tso's chicken."

"That's my favorite too!" squealed Mu Mu. "And their sliced pork with mixed vegetables!"

Before Olivia could think of anything to add, the cashier returned and called out, "Lin?"

Mu Mu shouted, "Right here!" as he handed her three filled-to-the-brim plastic bags. Trying not to stare, Olivia remembered Alex mentioning that Mu Mu had an enormous appetite. Actually, "big eater" was how her BFF put it.

"Got to run, company's coming," Mu Mu said with a smile. "See you at camp! Can't wait!"

"Right!" said Olivia, trying to match Mu Mu's enthusiasm.

CHAPTER 7

An easy silence fell between Olivia and her mother as they picked up their order and drove home. They decided to eat on the wraparound front porch that faced the Parkway. As they settled down, Sullivan waited patiently under the round wicker table.

"I have to order some new supplies for the shop," Olivia's mom started saying as she passed Olivia the carton of General Tso's chicken.

"New supplies like what?" Olivia asked, taking a serving.

"Oh, beads, lanyard laces, waxed cords, pearl cotton, charms. We already got in an expanded assortment of embroidery threads. Everybody wants them, especially your friend Ethan Fleckman. He keeps requesting so many different colors."

"He's not my friend," replied Olivia, picking up the last of the spareribs.

"Really? He always talks about you and Alex," her mom pointed out.

"Stop!" cried Olivia. "I'm eating."

"Well, in any event, we're going to have to order more friendship bracelet books too. We're getting a lot of requests for new patterns," her mother said, wiping her hands.

At the mention of friendship bracelets, Olivia remembered the one she had found in her mother's dresser, the mysterious blue-and-white one. She wondered, *Is now a good time to bring that up?*

"Of course, today, there are so many new patterns and threads," her mom continued. "I wonder if kids realize how popular friendship bracelets have been for years and years."

Before she could stop herself, Olivia blurted out, "OK, Mom, I saw that blue pouch with the friendship bracelet in your drawer. What's so special about it?"

For an instant, her mom appeared so distressed that

Olivia wondered if she'd said the wrong thing. Then her mom said in a low voice, "Everything. Everything is special about it."

"Mom, 'everything' sounds pretty dramatic," laughed Olivia. "Why is it special? Does it have magic powers?"

Her mother took out the pouch from her pants pocket. "Magic powers? Yes, I guess you could say it has magic powers." She opened the pouch and reached inside for the bracelet. "The magic of this friendship bracelet is how it led to the craft store."

"Katonah Crafts?" asked Olivia.

Her mother nodded. "It means a lot to me. When I was a little older than you, I had to have an operation, and a nice person gave me this bracelet."

Olivia gasped. "What kind of an operation?" She didn't know anything about an operation!

"I dove into the side of a pool and injured my spine. I was showing off for a group of kids...kids I thought I wanted to be friends with."

"Oh, Mom! Why didn't you ever tell me?"

"Because I got over it," said her mother, looking at

the bracelet entwined in her hands. "I wore this bracelet every day and even learned how to make others while I was getting better."

"You said a nice person gave you this bracelet. Who was that?" asked Olivia, still amazed.

"A girl named Dawn. Really, I didn't even know her that well. She had a twin sister, Nicole, and they were very, very close. Dawn came to visit me in the hospital totally out of the blue. She told me their parents went through a really terrible divorce and that she had to come here to New York to live with her father and Nicole had to stay in Texas with her mother."

Olivia looked shocked.

"I know. It seems cruel today," her mother explained. "And this was way before cell phones and email, so you can imagine how wrenching it was to be separated. Dawn missed her sister so much that her grades went down and she lost interest in practically everything."

"That's horrible!"

"Yes, but one day, Dawn got a letter in the mail with this bracelet. Nicole had made it for her with a wish that

Dawn would get better. Dawn told me that one small thing like that just made a huge difference."

"Wow!" said Olivia. "Amazing!" After a few seconds, she asked, "But what did you mean about the crafts shop?"

"That's how I fell in love with making things, really how I came to start Katonah Crafts. Sweetheart, if you want this bracelet, it's yours. Daddy and I love you so much and know that you will be able to make true friends again—friends as true as Alex."

"Tie it on for me?" asked Olivia, holding out her wrist.

Sullivan got up, walked over, sniffed it, and then tried to bite it.

"Stop!" Olivia told him while taking a better look at the bracelet. "But I'm not sure I remember what light blue means."

"Funny you should say that. Miss Ruth Ann is making up a chart for the shop with the meanings of all the colors. Light blue stands for loyalty," replied her mom, standing up. "I'm getting juice. Can I get you a glass?"

"Sure. But can I have that last spring roll?" asked Olivia, reaching into the carton. She was so intent on eating with her chopsticks that she didn't notice when a black Land Rover drove past their porch and turned at the corner onto Bedford Road. Out of sight, it drove down the green and then circled around to Alex's old house.

A boy and a girl jumped out of the backseat and headed inside.

The boy was tan with golden curls. It was Surfer Dude.

CHAPTER 8

Zoe Santana instantly fell in love with her new house on Bedford Road. Shaded by ancient chestnut trees, the old-fashioned house had fireplaces, window seats, and cozy nooks—just about everything she'd ever dreamed of.

But it was her new bedroom she especially loved, with its big bay window that faced the leafy backyard. *I love the color too*, she thought, surprising herself. Even though she would never have picked something girlie like lavender, there, in that airy space, it felt just right.

She walked across the pale-blue wall-to-wall carpeting and opened a door. The walk-in closet was gigantic! On the inside of the closet door was a full-length mirror.

So, this is what I look like in my new room, she thought. Reflected was an athletic-looking girl with tawny skin and long, dark curls held back with a headband. Her green eyes were framed with eyelashes so black and full she'd never have to worry about mascara.

Her mother walked in, saw Zoe gazing in the mirror, and smiled. "*Niña*," Zoe's mother said. "It's time to unpack." Behind her was a burly moving man pushing a hand truck loaded with cartons.

Zoe knew it would be useless to think about anything else until the unpacking was done.

Actually, she was kind of a pro at moving. This time, the move was because her mother had been appointed the new school superintendent in a large school district across the New York border, in Connecticut.

But this move was different. For one thing, it promised to be permanent. Zoe's mother had a long-term contract. For another, Zoe's new stepfather, Press, wrote a popular food blog from home. He'd said he was happy anywhere there was a decent gas stove.

In the past, Zoe had never let anyone know how hard it was to move. Fortunately for her, from an early age, she'd been an ace at soccer and softball. Just as she'd learned to walk off injuries on the field, when it came time to pack and say good-bye, she'd just walked off the pain.

"And Austen will be here soon to help out," her mother added.

Zoe hadn't seen her cousin Austen for a couple of years. So when he and her uncle Russell had picked her up last night at the Westchester Airport, she was amazed how good-looking he had become—tall, with golden curls framing his face.

She unpacked her tennis racket and took a brisk practice swing.

Hear he's supposed to be pretty good at tennis, she thought. *Let's see what he's got.*

CHAPTER 9

The afternoon was sunny and mild, so when her flute lesson ended, Olivia was happy to be outside, riding home on her bike.

Maybe I'll stop at the library and ask when Mrs. Vreeland has time to talk about volunteering, she thought. Making the sharp turn onto Bedford Road, she spotted a huge moving van parked in front of Alex's old house.

Moving van! She was so surprised, she didn't see the forty-foot-tall telephone pole in front of her until she crashed into it.

A tall boy and a dark-haired girl came running over. "Are you OK?" they asked.

Sprawled out facedown, Olivia felt totally embarrassed. The boy knelt down and helped her to her feet.

Her legs were covered with grass clippings. She brushed them off and then unfastened her bike helmet, letting her long hair fall over her shoulders.

"Hey, you're the girl from tennis camp," said the boy.

Then she looked his way. *Oh, great. I got my wish,* thought Olivia, immediately recognizing Surfer Dude. *But really, can I just die this minute?*

"Oh, right," she managed to reply. "Sorry I'm such a klutz."

"I'm Austen, and this is my cousin Zoe," the boy replied with a smile.

"I can't tell you how many times I've done things like that," Zoe said.

"Really?" asked Olivia. "No, not really. You're just saying that, right?"

Zoe laughed again. "You know, you're the first person I've met here. What's your name?"

"Here? You mean here? Here in Katonah here?" said Olivia, her voice rising. "Or here in this house here?" She pointed to Alex's house.

"Both. I'm moving in here with my mom and new dad."

"This was my best friend Alex's house," Olivia blurted out. "She just moved."

"It's pretty cool," said Austen. "Like a hundred years old?"

Olivia couldn't think of what to say. She felt like her whole BFF-moving story was such a downer, and she just met these kids.

"So Alex's best friend, are you going to tell us your name or not?" asked Zoe with a smile.

"Sorry," said Olivia, apologizing again. "I'm Olivia, Olivia Jones. I live on the Parkway. That's the street just up Bedford Road and around the corner from the library." She waved toward the top of the road.

"I live in North Salem," explained Austen. "That's probably why I've never seen you around. I went to Meadowlark Elementary. Do you go to Village Elementary?"

"Not anymore," said Olivia. "I'm going to Alexander Hamilton Middle School in September."

"Hey, me too," said Austen.

"And me," added Zoe.

"Sixth grade!" all three said at once.

The beauty of coincidence washed over Olivia, making her feel better. "Well, all I can say is cool!"

The three middle schoolers started to laugh.

"Kids, you want to move out of the way?" said one of the moving men unloading an elliptical trainer.

Austen steered the girls onto the sidewalk. "We were just going to Main Street so Zoe can check out the crafts shop. You want to come with us?" he asked Olivia.

Nice! thought Olivia, nodding her head yes. *I'll go to the library later.*

As she leaned down to pick up her bike, she noticed that Austen was wearing a friendship bracelet around his ankle. The pattern was awesome, with diamonds and *X*'s and *O*'s. *What meanings can those colors have: dark blue, light green, and orange?*

"I want to get some threads so I can try that pattern," Zoe was telling him while pointing to the bracelet. "Do you think the crafts store has them?" she asked.

"Probably," he replied. "I went in there earlier, but some dude was hogging all the space around the threads.

Hey, Zoe, look. Olivia has a friendship bracelet too. Blue and white—cool colors."

"I know Katonah Crafts has lots of supplies for friendship bracelets," said Olivia. "My mom owns the shop."

Zoe and Austen broke out in big smiles.

"That's so cool," said Zoe, putting her phone away. "I just texted my mom. Let's go!"

Austen turned to Olivia. "Here, let me walk your bike for you," he said.

She thanked him with a smile and couldn't help thinking that, sometimes, being a klutz paid off.

CHAPTER 10

"I really want something that's brighter orange than Thermo," a voice familiar to Olivia was saying. "Saturday is the earliest you can get in the metallic threads?"

When the three walked into Katonah Crafts, Ethan Fleckman was studying the Dyno Threads catalog with Miss Ruth Ann.

Olivia's heart sank. *Please, please, don't let him call me any gross names in front of Austen and Zoe*, she prayed.

"Oh, hello, dear," said Miss Ruth Ann to Olivia. Then, she lowered her glasses and looked up at Austen with interest. "Weren't you just here a little while ago?" she asked him.

"Yes, I was," he said, throwing a look at Ethan. "But it was crowded, so I came back."

"Miss Ruth Ann, this is Zoe and her cousin Austen," said Olivia, introducing them. "Guess what? Zoe's family is moving into Alex's old house."

"That's nice. Welcome to Katonah," said Miss Ruth Ann.

"Alex's house? What happened to her?" interrupted Ethan, looking startled.

"They moved to Paris?" replied Olivia, who wanted to say what he would have: "Duh, where have you been?" But instead, she turned to Zoe and Austen. "This is Ethan Fleckman. He's in my class," she said. "I mean our class."

"Hi," said Ethan, barely looking at them. "Yeah, but is Alex coming back soon?" he asked Olivia.

"No, they *moved*. Why?"

For once Ethan seemed to be speechless.

"Olivia, why don't you show your friends around the shop while we finish here?" Miss Ruth Ann quickly said.

Olivia nodded like that was a good idea and steered Zoe and Austen toward the embroidery and craft threads section, where there was a small round table and chairs. Austen immediately sat down and stretched out.

"This place is so cool, Olivia," said Zoe, picking up a pattern book. "Has your mom had it for long?" She thumbed through a few pages and then pulled out a chair.

"Ever since I can remember," replied Olivia, sitting down too. "She's in the city right now, at the crafts show, checking out what's new."

Austen reached over and untied the friendship bracelet from his ankle. "So, Zoe, maybe Miss Ruth Ann can tell you where to find the pattern for this?" he asked her. "Didn't you want to make one?"

Before Zoe could reply, a voice said, "It's the Mega Diamond XXOO pattern. Where did you get it?"

Austen looked up at Ethan. "Where did I get it? My brother gave it to me," Austen said with a little coolness in his voice.

"Well, it's advanced," replied Ethan. "Super advanced."

"I'll tell him you said that." Austen laughed.

Ethan looked flustered for a brief moment, and then he laughed too. "OK," he said. Turning to Zoe, he added,

"The pattern is in the *Galaxy* book, over there on the top shelf. If you need help, text me. Here's my number."

"Sure," said Zoe, pulling out her phone. "And what's yours, Olivia?"

All four started sharing their info. Olivia was a little surprised Ethan took hers.

"OK. Got it. See you," he said after a minute. He stood up and reached behind the counter for his skateboard. "Hey, Olivia," he said before leaving. "If you want this, it's yours." He tossed her something and then walked out.

Olivia snagged it with one hand and then looked down.

It was a pink friendship bracelet with hearts and the name *Alex* in the middle.

OMG! she realized. *Ethan was going to give this to Alex. She was his secret crush!*

CHAPTER 11

"*Oui! Oui!* Yes, yes, Alex. It's your old house. Zoe's parents bought your house. Can you believe that?" Olivia reported the next morning on Skype. Because it was six hours later in Paris than in New York in the summer, she'd had to wait overnight to share all the huge, huge 411: the house news, the Austen news, the crazy Ethan Fleckman/friendship bracelet news.

"Ollie, no! Our house... That is so weird. Did you go inside?"

"Nope," Olivia replied.

"Uh-oh, I have to go. Papa's friends just walked in. They have a daughter my age, but I want to hear more later. Au revoir!"

"Au revoir."

"Ollie?"

She looked up to see her dad coming in with Sullivan.

"Let's go up to the town courts," he said, rubbing his hands together in anticipation. "I want to try out my new racket. Come on, on your feet."

Olivia immediately jumped up, eager to play. She always got in the best workouts with her dad because he was so fast and didn't just let her win. "OK, I'm almost ready. I just have to walk Sully."

"You didn't do that yet?" he replied, trying to look stern but missing by a mile. "Make it snappy. You know how crowded the courts get on the weekends."

"OK, Dad. Be right back," she replied, heading toward the front porch. "Come on, Sully."

As Sullivan pulled her around the corner from the Parkway onto Bedford Road, Olivia had a view straight down the town green, with a good view of Alex's old house. *Oh, wow, there's Zoe*, she thought, watching her new friend step out onto her front porch and hold open the front door. "Zoe, Zoe!" she shouted but then stopped.

Because Elin Pierson was walking right behind Zoe.

Immediately, Olivia dived behind a bushy pine tree, yanking Sullivan behind her. *I feel like a spy*, she thought, slowly pulling apart two branches and peeking out. There was Elin, tucking her super-long blond hair into a baby-blue bike helmet. She hopped on her bike, the one with the blue streamers and white basket, and Zoe followed.

Uh-oh, this can't be good news, Olivia thought, letting go of the branches. Too late, she realized the branches would spring back and swipe her in the face. "Ooh, that hurts!" she cried. "Come on, Sully," she added with tears in her eyes.

After that, Olivia's morning got a little better because the town park wasn't crowded when they drove up in her dad's ancient Land Cruiser, the car he would never part with despite its having well over three hundred thousand miles.

Itching to nail down an empty court, her dad hopped out first. "See you inside, kiddo," he said over his shoulder. "Try to keep up."

Olivia broke into a jog and had almost made it past the bike racks when Zoe rode in with Elin.

"Hey, Olivia," cried Zoe, taking off her helmet. "I thought that was you."

Olivia stopped for a minute. "Yup, I'm here with my dad," she replied, pointing to the courts. "Hi, Elin," she said.

"Oh, hi there," Elin replied in a flat voice.

Olivia noticed that Elin was wearing a perky pink-and-white tennis outfit with pink sneakers. *Sort of like a cheerleader look*, Olivia thought. Then she remembered her own outfit—cutoffs and an old tank top with a rainbow on the front. Right away she thought, *Why didn't I change? This is so grungy and babyish.*

"We might meet Austen up here too," said Zoe.

Ping! Olivia felt a little dart in her heart. "Really? That's super," she said, trying to sound normal. "I better go catch up with Dad. Bye."

"Bye," said Zoe.

"Bye, Elin," added Olivia, running off.

She was almost on the court when it hit her.

Along with those girlie pink sneakers, Elin was wearing a familiar-looking friendship bracelet: the Mega

Diamond XXOO pattern in dark blue, light green, and orange. It looked a whole lot like the super advanced one Austen said his brother gave him.

She stormed past her dad, grabbed her racket, and took up her position. Feeling incredibly freaked out, she told herself, *I am so going to tear up this court.*

CHAPTER 12

Give me the total 411, Ollie. XXXOOO

That's cool, thought Olivia when she saw Alex's text. With a smile, she plunked down on the window seat in her bedroom with Sullivan, who was busy working on a rawhide chew.

There was simply too much news to text. She would be there typing for a week. Instead, she spelled out, Skype tomorrow? XXXOOO and rested the phone on her legs.

Super, now there was something good to look forward to, because tomorrow afternoon, she had an appointment with Dr. Justin, the orthodontist. That promised to be just awful. "Your crossbite is getting worse," Olivia's mom decided. "Nobody wants braces, but you'll thank me when you're older."

When I'm way older, thought Olivia at the time, *because there's no way I am going to thank anybody now.*

Her feet ached from running hard at the courts earlier, where she actually beat her dad in one game, so she stretched out her legs and propped them up on Sully. Just lolling there, staring out the window, she started to feel bummed out again. No Alex, Elin Pierson and Austen's stupid friendship bracelet, and the possibility of braces? *Can things get any worse?*

Woof! Woof! Woof! Without warning, Sullivan burst into ferocious barks and bounded off the bed. Her phone went flying across the room.

"Olivia! Olivia!" her mother called. "Come downstairs."

"What is it, Mom?" she said, hurrying over to the bannister.

"You have a guest. Ethan Fleckman is here."

With a sigh, she started to walk slowly downstairs.

CHAPTER 13

Thank heavens for the wisteria vine on the front porch, because Olivia didn't have a clue why Ethan was there, and if she stood in the shadows, no one would see her. Because, seriously, Ethan dropping in like that was super weird!

Before Olivia could even say hello, he told her, "I thought you could give these to Zoe." He hoisted his backpack onto the corner table and unbuckled it. Olivia couldn't help noticing it was the red bag with the image of a fierce white shark printed on the front. She remembered how Ethan started a fad with that backpack last year in fifth grade. And that was also totally weird because before that, honestly, nobody ever paid much attention to him.

He handed her a few sheets of paper precisely stapled together. It took only a quick glance for her to make out that they were instructions for friendship bracelets, including one for the Mega Diamond XXOO pattern like Austen's.

"Can't you give them to Zoe yourself? You do know she lives in Alex's old house?" she asked, worried she'd run into Zoe's new sidekick, Elin Magic Tresses.

Ethan looked uncomfortable. "Yeah but maybe you can give them to her?" he repeated.

Olivia picked up on his uneasiness. "OK," she said and started to check out the instructions. But after a few seconds, she said, "Ethan, they're all marked up?"

"I know," he replied. "I figured out easier ways to make them. You know, like shortcuts?"

Guess he wants to be sure Zoe contacts him for help. Nobody could possibly read this scribbly mess, Olivia figured. "OK, cool," she told him.

A dead silence fell between them. Olivia could hear the drone of a Weedwacker down the block. "Thanks, Ethan," she finally said.

At the same moment, he started saying, "So I thought you and Alex used to like making bracelets too. Didn't you get some purple and white threads from your mom's shop to make twin bracelets?"

"Oh, yeah," replied Olivia. Why hadn't she realized how much Ethan hung around Katonah Crafts when she was there with Alex?

"I could help you finish them," he offered right away.

"Don't have to. They're done," she explained, holding up her left arm, where she had tied on Alex's bracelet earlier that morning, right next to her blue-and-white one from her mom.

There was another awkward moment of silence, and then when he still didn't reply, she tried to bail. "I'll take these to Zoe later," she said, pointing to the instruction sheets and then inching closer to the porch door.

The screen door flew open in her face, and Sullivan came prancing out, followed by her mom, who was carrying two bottles of water.

"Thought you kids might be thirsty," she said in a

bright voice. Sullivan jumped all over Ethan like he was his new best friend.

Olivia shot her mom a quick look, a sort of *What are you doing?* look.

Her mother just smiled and put down the bottles on the round table next to Ethan's shark backpack. "Now, Ethan, what are you up to this summer?" she asked. "You always seem to be busy."

As if he had been dying of thirst, Ethan lunged for a bottle of water. "Thanks, Mrs. Jones," he said, unscrewing the top and taking a long swallow. "Actually, I wanted to ask you something about flosses, but it can wait until tomorrow, when Katonah Crafts is open."

"No, no, of course not," Olivia's mom replied. "Ask me now. It's so great to see young people doing such creative things. Isn't it, Ollie?"

Olivia nodded yes to be polite and once again tried to get away. Reading her daughter's mind, her mom put her arm around Olivia's shoulder to keep her there. "What is it you need, Ethan?" she asked.

He took another swallow of water and then said all in

a rush, "Well, I'm trying to start a club to make friendship bracelets for kids at Central Hospital. I was there on Friday to visit my cousin, and the kids were, like, super bored."

Before he could even finish his sentence, Olivia's mom exclaimed, "That's an absolutely wonderful idea!"

"Yeah, but I need some help," Ethan continued.

"Katonah Crafts will give you all the supplies you need!" Olivia's mom promised right away. "We would be delighted to." Then she turned to Olivia. "And, sweetie, wouldn't you like to be a part of this? Ethan, do you have other volunteers or club members?"

"No, I wanted to ask you first," Ethan said rapidly. "I mean, if it's OK about the supplies?"

"Yes, yes, we would very much like to sponsor that. And I'll drive you whenever you need to go or make arrangements for transportation. But really, the hospital is so close, you could ride your bikes there. Well, whatever. This is a wonderful idea. Isn't it, Olivia?" her mom said once more.

Actually, it is a good idea, Olivia admitted to herself. *I'm kind of amazed Ethan thought of it.*

"Right, Mom," she agreed with a smile. "It's super

cool. But, uh, do you want me to help too? I could kick in some of my birthday money?"

"Maybe you could be in the club?" he suggested instead, surprising her. "I mean, help make bracelets and drop them off at the hospital? Or even show some of the kids there how to make them?"

"Sure," she replied. "Anything else?"

Sullivan jumped up on Ethan again, wagging his tail. "Look, he wants to be club mascot," Olivia joked, while pulling him down. "Sorry, Sully, you cannot go to the hospital," she told him.

Ethan stood there looking blank. *Guess he doesn't go for the warm and fuzzy*, thought Olivia.

Her mom loved this club/hospital idea and seemed eager to get things rolling. "Well, how would you like to start tomorrow? We can meet at Katonah Crafts at nine o'clock, before it opens. Ollie, remember, we have the orthodontist at eleven."

Ethan and Olivia nodded in agreement.

"OK! That's settled. And what will you call your club, Ethan? You do need a name," Olivia's mom pointed out.

"Don't know," he said, shooting Olivia a look. "Aren't you the one who's supposed to be so good at English?"

Olivia gazed above them, noticing the hundreds of tendrils of the old wisteria vine and thought, *They've wrapped themselves together to make one strong vine. Kind of like how threads are knotted together to make a friendship bracelet.*

"How about THREADS?" she suggested. "You know, all these different threads that come together: the bracelets, the kids, and us?"

"Cool. Yeah, THREADS is seriously cool," agreed Ethan, packing up his water bottle. "I have to go. See you tomorrow?"

He swung his red-and-white backpack over his shoulder. "And, Olivia, you can ask Zoe to be in THREADS too if you want. BTW, I put a couple of my old friendship bracelets in her mailbox yesterday. One was like Austen's. Maybe you can tell her they're there?"

"I think she found them already, Ethan," Olivia said, smiling. She was so relieved to learn that the bracelet Elin was wearing wasn't from Austen. *Zoe probably gave it to her*, she thought. *Or more likely, Elin just asked for it. After all, she just asked for free samples that day in Katonah Crafts.*

"OK, bye," said Ethan, picking up his skateboard and gliding down the front walk.

"Don't worry. I'll tell Zoe ASAP," she called after him.

CHAPTER 14

It was so, so beyond strange for Olivia to actually ring the bell after a lifetime of just walking straight into her BFF's house. But things had changed. It was Zoe's house now, and Olivia pressed the buzzer once more. She knew the ring was loud, so somebody should hear it.

When nobody answered after a few minutes, she headed back down the front walk. Right away, she got into her worry zone. *Maybe Elin told Zoe not to bother with me?* But just as quickly, she replaced that thought with a more realistic one: *Zoe's parents have company. There are cars parked in the driveway and a few in front of the house. They're probably in the back and didn't hear the bell.*

Whew, good save, she thought, walking a little faster.

The last thing she wanted to do was barge in on a party. But before she could get too far away, she heard Zoe.

"Olivia! Olivia!" she was yelling out, and then she sprinted up Bedford Road toward her.

Wow! Zoe is a super-fast runner, Olivia realized when, seconds later, her new friend was standing before her.

"Thought I heard the doorbell. Hey, what's up?" asked Zoe.

"Oh, I wanted to drop off something for you, from Ethan, Ethan Fleckman," she explained, digging in her backpack for the papers.

Zoe gazed down at them. "They're instruction sheets for friendship bracelets, right? You know, I found a ton of bracelets in the mailbox. They were from Ethan? There were so many. This girl Elin asked for one, so I gave it to her. My mom and I met her in a place called Magic Tresses. She said her mother owns it? Oh, yeah, you saw us up at the town park this morning. But what are all these notes?" she asked, pointing to the scribbling.

Olivia laughed. "They're Ethan's shortcuts. He's pretty good at stuff like that."

"Super. I'll text him. But first, come on into the backyard. We're having a cookout," Zoe urged her. "Preston, my new father, is grilling ribs, baby back ribs. He's trying out Rosario's, that Italian butcher shop on Main Street?"

"Rosario's? My dad always goes there. But why don't I text you later?" Olivia suggested, still reluctant to break in on Zoe's family gathering.

"Come on," said Zoe, pulling her by the arm. "It's not like you haven't been in the backyard before."

Olivia knew every rock and stone, every shrub, tree, and flower as well as she knew her own face. Only now, there was a different set of bright outdoor furniture on the big flagstone patio and different group of people— people she'd never seen before. She couldn't help thinking, *This day is getting weirder and weirder.*

Zoe had on a big smile. Olivia could tell she was super happy about her new home. "Come meet Mama. Mama, this is Olivia Jones, the girl I told you about," Zoe called out to her mother.

Zoe's mother turned around and smiled too. Then she walked over to them and extended a hand. "Olivia, welcome to our new home. But this must feel so peculiar to you. Zoe told us this was your best friend's house, the friend who moved to Paris?"

"Yes, it was," admitted Olivia. Then she added in a halting voice, "Excuse me, I don't mean to be rude, but I don't know what to call you. Zoe says she has a new father?"

Zoe laughed and put her arm around her mother's shoulder. "We were just talking about that! Mama has a different last name from me. She's Lopez, Dr. Lopez, and I'm Santana. Oh, and here's Preston, my new father. He's a MacNab."

A tall man with a short, reddish beard ambled over. Olivia immediately liked his eyes that crinkled at the edges and looked as sharp as a bird's. "Yes, the Irish are outnumbered here," he told Olivia with a laugh. "But any pets we get will be MacNabs and male. Zoe's mother has promised me that."

"Pets!" cried Zoe, electrified as her face lit up. "Are we getting a pet, Mama?"

"Let's settle in first, Niña," cautioned Zoe's mother,

holding her hands in the air in the "wait up" gesture, "and then we'll review our options."

The light in Zoe's face faded, but she didn't freak out. *She's too cool to lose it in front of people*, thought Olivia, impressed.

"Hey, kiddo, don't look so sad," her stepfather said. "That's academic talk for yes."

"Really?" asked Zoe, perking up again.

"Press!" said Dr. Lopez, shaking her head. "What are you thinking?"

"Gotta get back to those ribs," he said, trying to get himself out of trouble.

"Just a minute, you," laughed Dr. Lopez, grabbing him by his apron. "You let the genie out of the bottle. Now you deal with it."

"Honey, those ribs are gonna burn," replied Mr. MacNab with a laugh.

Zoe's mother shook her head and turned to Zoe. "What would you like, Niña? A kitten brother or a puppy brother?"

Olivia knew how she would answer that. The day her

dad had brought home ten-week-old Sullivan was the happiest day of her life.

"I get to decide? Wow! I'll think, I'll think, I'll think about it. Thanks, Mama. Thanks, Press," Zoe said, laughing and giving each of them a hug.

"That's great," said Olivia. "Seriously."

"Do you have a pet?" Zoe's mother asked her.

"Yes, a two-year-old golden retriever named Sullivan. He's so sweet. But he's pretty frisky. Mom says he's high energy."

"High energy? So is Zoe," said her stepfather. "Maybe Zoe can meet him sometime?"

"Sure," replied Olivia, thinking, *What will Dad say when he finds out Sullivan might be a role model?*

"Hey, Zoe, what do you look so happy about?" Olivia heard someone ask.

Austen was coming toward them with a big bowl in his hands. "Uncle Press, here's your coleslaw," he announced, putting the bowl down on a long picnic table. "Hey, Olivia. Cool, you're here," he said, catching sight of her. "Like your rainbow shirt. My sister, Becky, has one just like it."

Oh no! With horror, Olivia realized she was still in the same clothes she'd played tennis in. *You know what?* she said to herself. *You are definitely going to have to step up your game. New clothes, ASAP!*

"Hi, Austen. Zoe just got some good news," she said with a smile. Then she quickly closed her mouth. *OMG! What if he saw my crossbite? What if everybody sees my crossbite?*

"Super!" he replied. "What?"

"Come on back to the swings, and I'll tell you all about it," laughed Zoe.

Just then, a toddler with a head of golden curls ran over, "Gus, Gus," she cried, reaching up to Austen.

"Olivia, this is Becky, my little sister," he said, hoisting her on his shoulders for a piggyback ride. "Becky, say hello."

Ouch! Becky did have a rainbow T-shirt too, Olivia realized. The little girl was wearing it.

CHAPTER 15

Dr. Justin's waiting room was *so* crowded. Olivia and her mother had been there for forty-five minutes already, and Olivia couldn't stop wishing she had her phone, but her mom made her leave it home.

"You have to turn it off in the doctor's office anyway," she'd pointed out when they were getting ready to make the short drive to the Medical Arts Building.

"Mom, I'm super bored," whispered Olivia, trying to adjust her long legs into a more comfortable position. Her new lime-green skinny jeans felt snug, but she was determined to dress better. "These magazines are ancient...and didn't that kid come in after us?" A boy of about seven went past them on his way to the inner office. He had that slow shuffle kids used when they dreaded going somewhere. His father was practically dragging him in.

"Just be patient," her mom whispered back. Then she tried to change the subject. "The meeting of THREADS went well this morning," she pointed out.

"It wasn't much of a meeting, Mom, just Ethan and me," replied Olivia. "I wish I had brought some supplies so I could work on a bracelet here."

The day before, at Zoe's family cookout, Olivia had told Zoe and Austen all about THREADS. Right away, the two cousins jumped onboard, but on such short notice, they couldn't make the first meeting. *Bummer*, Olivia had thought, so it was just her and Ethan the next morning when Olivia's mom opened Katonah Crafts and flicked on the lights.

Then, to make it worse, Ethan seemed less than thrilled when she told him about Austen.

Ethan had been checking out his list of colors and patterns. "Yeah, well, Zoe wants to make bracelets, but Austen wasn't too interested the other day in actually making anything," he pointed out.

"How do you know that?" Olivia had asked, feeling bad that she hadn't thought about Ethan's reaction, and she had to admit, THREADS was his idea. She had to find a way to make it OK. How could she possibly tell Austen he couldn't be in the club now?

Olivia had sat at the crafts table and pondered the situation. Then, she'd realized something. "Hey, Ethan, yesterday, Austen told me his mother works at Central Hospital," she explained. "Don't we need their permission to visit the patients? Maybe that's one way Austen can help?"

"Guess so," Ethan said with zero enthusiasm.

"Good thinking," agreed Olivia's mom from across the shop. "Of course, this is your project," she quickly added and then reached for her tote. "I'm going out to Katonah Beans for coffee. Can you tell Miss Ruth Ann when she gets in? She just texted that she's parking her car now. And who would like cocoa? We can have it on the stoop outside."

"My mom never allows any food in the shop," Olivia explained to Ethan.

Ethan shot her one of his "duh" looks and said, "You do know that I have been here before. But OK, let's meet with Zoe and Austen tomorrow. Can they be here at ten o'clock, when the shop opens?"

"I'll ask Zoe," Olivia had replied, a little relieved.

Dr. Justin's office was finally thinning out. Olivia was desperate. *I can't possibly reread this year-old copy of* The Smithsonian *magazine*, she thought. Or spend another minute looking at the Smile Board with before and after photos of patients. She'd already told her mom she didn't want her photo up there. No way. But she was surprised by how many kids she recognized.

She caved and reached for the magazine when the door to the outer hallway opened and in flew Mu Mu Lin.

"Olivia!" she cried. "Wow! You come here too? First Golden Panda, now Dr. Justin?"

"Right, right," Olivia said with a smile, happy to see a friend.

"Hi, Mrs. Jones," said Mu Mu, turning to Olivia's mother. "My mom is outside," she said, pointing in the direction of the parking lot, "in the car, talking to her office, as usual. She can't be without her phone. Oh, gosh, have you been here long? It's always this way, right?"

Mu Mu's energy revived Olivia. "Yes, and I think I've learned all I can about endangered inchworms," she joked, putting the magazine back on the table.

"LOL!" said Mu Mu with a big laugh. "So, why are you here? I've got a crossbite and Mom wants me to get braces. She says I'll thank her. Yuck!"

Olivia's mom couldn't help overhearing that and immediately tried to bury her face in last month's *Highlights* magazine.

Mu Mu plunked down next to Olivia and untied her backpack. "Do you want a Fruit Roll-Up or some gummy worms?" she whispered, reaching into the bag.

"Oh, no thanks. I think I'm next," said Olivia, trying to hide her shock that Mu Mu would bring food to an orthodontist appointment, much less gummy worms.

"Better stock up now," Mu Mu advised, "'cause once those braces go on, good-bye, caramels, popcorn, bagels, pistachios, everything good." She rolled her eyes, sighed, and took out a baggie filled with what looked like home-made chocolate-chip cookies.

Olivia had to smile. *Alex was right. Mu Mu is fun*, she thought. *She's certainly not afraid to say what she's thinking. Maybe she would like to be in THREADS? No, no! No more new members without talking to Ethan.*

"Olivia!" cried out the receptionist. "Please go into exam room two. Dr. Justin will be with you shortly."

"Good luck!" shouted Mu Mu as Olivia headed toward the inner office. "And don't forget: brace yourself! Ha-ha!"

"We're not totally sure I'll need braces. Hope not," Olivia replied, holding up her crossed fingers high in the air.

CHAPTER 16

"Oh no, Ollie. I'm so sorry! How long do you have to wear them?"

"Just forever to eternity," replied Olivia.

Alex laughed. "Don't be so dramatic. Seriously, for how long?"

"Dr. Justin said about a year, about long enough to ruin my life. He said my crossbite is not that bad."

"Well, that's good. Can you pick the color braces?"

"They gave me a chart, but who cares? I mean, I have to think about it," Olivia replied, trying to sound as if she could handle the situation.

"Blue would match your eyes," Alex pointed out. "And pink is pretty too."

"Cool. Text me later. Love you!" said Olivia. She

clicked off and then headed to her bedroom, where she'd left the color chart. Overwhelmed by this newest bummer, she couldn't help thinking, *I just want to stay in bed for the rest of the day. Possibly for the rest of my life...*

Her phone buzzed with a text from Zoe. Going to look @ puppies. Come over now!

As if she were hit with a happiness bolt, instantly she felt one thousand times better. Quickly, she slipped into her new knit top with the graphic of a dream catcher and then put her long hair up in a fresh ponytail.

"Mom, I'm going to Zoe's," she cried, heading to the front door. "They're going to look at puppies!"

"Have fun and be careful!" her mom replied.

All the way down Bedford Road, Olivia couldn't stop thinking, *Maybe it's a golden retriever puppy? That would be so cool!*

CHAPTER 17

Zoe'd never had a pet before. Until her mother married Press, it had always been just her and Mama. She knew that a puppy meant Katonah really was going to be their home. Before, her mother had always made excuses like they needed a big yard or more room or she was too busy. But now with Press there, working a lot from home… He really wanted a dog too, she could tell. It just had to be the right dog.

She was so excited she couldn't stop chattering away as they drove deeper into the countryside, past Katonah and the Muscoot Reservoir, into the neighboring hamlet of Golden's Bridge. "You'll help me, right, Olivia? I mean give me tips, right? Oh, and we'll have to get him a collar and a leash…a bed and some toys. Puppies like toys, right?"

"Oh, right," said Olivia, remembering how sweet and tiny Sullivan was as a puppy—and how much work.

Zoe's mother turned around from the front passenger seat. "And we'll need some books on training. You should go to the library now and study up, so you are ready when the time comes," she pointed out. She was sitting next to Mr. MacNab, who was trying to follow the directions on a new GPS.

"It should be soon, Press," Zoe's mother said, scanning the road. "The breeder said it's right off Windmill Road, just past the restaurant. Look for the sign and turn left, probably in about fifty feet."

"In fifty feet, make the left turn at the sign," instructed the GPS lady's voice.

"OK, OK," laughed Zoe's father, slowing down. "It's really beautiful country up here," he observed. "Lots of farms and big spreads and this close to New York City."

"Make the left turn at the sign," repeated the GPS lady.

"Stop nagging!" Press told her, and Zoe's mother laughed.

Then she turned around to face Zoe again. "Now, Niña, do not let your hopes run away with your brain. I told you what Mrs. Mumford said, that all the puppies in this litter were already spoken for. We simply want to see if this is the right breed for us."

"Yes, Mama, yes," said Zoe, unable to keep the anticipation out of her voice. *At least this is the first step*, she thought.

Olivia looked at her new friend and was so happy for her—and really happy for herself. To be included in a puppy search? It doesn't get much better!

"How old was Sullivan when you got him, Olivia?" asked Zoe's stepfather.

"Ten weeks. A friend of my dad's in Connecticut had him first, but his little boy turned out to be allergic, so we got him instead," she explained.

"Press, slow down," said Dr. Lopez. "There's the sign up ahead."

Olivia looked out of the car window. "Golden's Bridge Goldens" said a white sign with a painting of a golden retriever puppy.

"You're getting a golden retriever!" she blurted out.

"Hope so. Didn't I tell you?" said Zoe.

"I was afraid to ask," replied Olivia. "What made you decide?" *It couldn't have been Zoe's visit late yesterday afternoon when Sullivan wouldn't stop jumping on her.*

"Tell you later. Come on, everybody!" cried Zoe, flinging open the car door.

Right in the middle of Mrs. Mumford's large, sunny family room, there was a low wire fence shaped into a circle. Inside it, the floor was covered with fresh layers of newspapers and pee pads.

Zoe's heart melted when she walked closer. The mother dog was on her side, and snoozing on top of her were six or seven of the cutest puppies ever, round, little fluff balls with light, almost-white fur. "Oh, they look like baby polar bears!" she cried.

"They're just waking up from nap time," explained Mrs. Mumford, a gray-haired woman who seemed very used to being in control. Actually, she reminded Olivia of Miss Ruth Ann. "Come, come, you can come over." She waved to them while scooping up a little, sleepy-eyed pup.

"This is a little girl," she said, pointing to the woven pink band around the puppy's neck. "My granddaughters love to make friendship bracelets, so they started making different-colored bands for the litters. That's so we can tell who's who. Now, this little one's name is Millie. Would you like to hold her?" she asked, handing the pup to Zoe.

Carefully, Zoe cradled the little dog in her arms. "She's so soft!" she exclaimed.

Dr. Lopez and Press leaned over to pet the puppy too. Olivia couldn't help noticing that they were all beaming. *Maybe this will be easier than Zoe realizes*, she thought. *Hope so.*

"And here is a little boy. We call him Carl," said Mrs. Mumford, handing Zoe's stepfather a puppy with a blue-and-white band. "He's the biggest in the litter by far. We expect he'll be a very big one."

"Really?" said Mr. MacNab with a big smile. He rubbed Carl's wide forehead and said, "Here, Zoe, you hold this bruiser," handing him over while Mrs. Mumford put Millie back in the enclosure.

"Wow! Yep, Carl is a lot heavier," laughed Zoe, taking the pup in her arms. "So you're the big one, you're the big one," she said, putting her finger in his mouth and gently shaking his jaw.

"How old are the puppies?" asked Olivia.

"Eight weeks today," the breeder replied.

"Oh, Carl, today is your birthday!" cried Zoe. "Happy birthday, little baby. He's so cute!" She gave him a hug.

"How long do people have to wait on your list for a puppy, Mrs. Mumford?" asked Zoe's mother.

"Usually about ten months or more, Dr. Lopez," she said.

Dr. Lopez raised her eyebrows. "And yesterday you said that all of the puppies in this particular litter have long been spoken for. Well, Niña, you will have to be very patient if you want a golden," she said.

"Yes, Mama," she replied, stroking Carl's big puppy feet.

Mrs. Mumford watched her and then said with a smile, "We always ask our families: Do you think you are ready for a dog like this? Goldens are wonderful but lively. They require work and care and lots of exercise."

"I'll do that! I'll exercise with the puppy," Zoe piped up.

"She plays soccer," Press explained. "Zoe is very athletic."

"That's good." Mrs. Mumford nodded. "And you know, actually the summer is an ideal time to bring Puppy home and train him."

Olivia looked down at the enclosure. All the baby dogs were now awake and tumbling over one another. *Poor Zoe, ten months will be one long wait*, she thought.

"Mrs. Mumford, may I pet the puppies?" she asked, kneeling down.

"Certainly. Now Dr. Lopez mentioned that you already have a golden?" she asked Olivia.

"Yes, Sullivan," she said, looking up. "He's almost two years old. We got him from a family in Connecticut who couldn't keep him."

Mrs. Mumford scooped up a pup with a yellow band and handed it to Olivia. "You can sit on the floor and play with this little one, if you like. Her name is Molly."

Olivia couldn't get over the resemblance to Sullivan.

"Is your golden light colored like these?" Mrs. Mumford asked.

The little pup was covering Olivia's face with kisses. "Yes," she managed to reply with a laugh.

Mrs. Mumford looked thoughtful. "I know most of the breeders in the area. Do you mind my asking the name of the person who gave you your dog?"

"It was a friend of my dad's, Captain Burke. He's a state police officer," Olivia explained, putting little Molly on her lap.

Mrs. Mumford was surprised. "Captain Burke! Why of course I know him and his family. They adopted a little boy from Trixie's first litter. Let me check my records," she said, opening her phone. "Yes, the puppy was part of a litter born two years ago this past June 21."

"June 21 is Sullivan's birthday!" cried Olivia. "Wow! So he came from here."

Mrs. Mumford put away her phone. "I'm so sorry the Burkes couldn't keep the puppy. They were a lovely family. But, of course, the dog has found a wonderful home with you," she added.

Olivia stroked Molly's warm, plump belly. "Is Sullivan, our dog, related to this litter?" she asked.

"Oh, yes, our female dogs only have a litter every two years or so," said Mrs. Mumford with a smile. "In fact, Sullivan has both the same parents as this litter—he's their older brother."

"What! That's amazing!" Olivia cried out. This was major! "Sullivan has brothers and sisters and Trixie is his mother? Oh, may I pet her?"

"Of course," replied Mrs. Mumford. With a smile, she reached for Molly as Olivia got to her feet.

"Oh, this is totally super. I'm getting to meet Sullivan's mother," Olivia said, petting the mother dog's head. "Trixie, your son Sullivan is a very good boy…most of the time!"

Everyone laughed at that.

Olivia asked, "Mrs. Mumford, may I take a photo for my parents?"

"Usually, we don't allow cameras in here," said Mrs. Mumford, "but this is special. Why don't you give me your phone, and I'll take some photos of you with Trixie?"

The cheerful living room fell silent as the breeder took

a few quick pics. "Good girl," said Olivia to Trixie when they were done.

Zoe looked up from petting Carl to see her mother shooting Press a look. He nodded back. She thought, *They're hooked. Yay! Now we have to add our name to the list. That's step number two.*

"Well, Mrs. Mumford, perhaps you will let us add our name to your waiting list?" Dr. Lopez asked the breeder.

Mrs. Mumford smiled and said, "Here is the situation. I can see you would be a very good family for one of our puppies. Usually we have one or two interviews before placing a pup. But we had a last-minute cancellation just this morning, and if you are ready to accept a puppy into your home, there is one available."

"Seriously?" exclaimed Zoe, her eyes opening wide. *We made it to step number three already?*

Carl was so relaxed he was snoozing on her shoulder. But he must have sensed Zoe's excitement because at that moment, he lifted his head and gave her a tiny puppy kiss on her cheek. Zoe was so touched, she practically cried in front of everyone. *Please let it be*

Carl, she prayed. *Press already loves him. And Mama. And me.*

Dr. Lopez had never seen her strong, quiet daughter display so much emotion. She turned to Press.

"May I ask which puppy is available?" he asked.

Mrs. Mumford walked over to Zoe. "Yes, it's this big fellow, Carl," she said, petting the puppy's head. "He's a good fit for you. He loves company and attention. If you wish, you may take him home now. He's had all his shots. Come into my office, and I'll give you a list of supplies, care instructions, food for a few days, and a blanket. Or would you prefer to go shopping today and pick him up tomorrow?"

"No! We'll take him now!" cried Zoe, cuddling him close.

"We have Sullivan's puppy crate!" cried Olivia. "Carl can have it!"

Zoe's parents laughed. "Well, I guess that's settled," said her mother with a smile. "Although this is happening very fast."

Press was smiling too. "Yes, it is. But let's go into your

office, Mrs. Mumford, and go over everything. Zoe, maybe you should be thinking of names, or is Carl the right one?"

"I love the name Carl," she answered right away. "Carlos Santana Lopez MacNab, that's who you are. Carl MacNab for short," she told the puppy.

"Carl it is," said Press, heading out of the room with Dr. Lopez and Mrs. Mumford. "We'll be back soon. Take care of him."

"We will!" the girls promised.

"Olivia, let's sit on the floor with him. I think Carl wants to play," said Zoe.

Olivia plopped down beside her and reached out for Carl. "Wow, Zoe, I can't believe you're getting a puppy today."

"*You* can't believe it?" replied Zoe. "I'm totally blown away!"

"And he's Sullivan's brother!" pointed out Olivia. "Wait till I tell my mom and dad."

"Look, Olivia," said Zoe, "Carl's neck band is the same pattern and colors as the friendship bracelet you're wearing."

Olivia looked down at the blue-and-white bracelet, the one her mom's friend Dawn made for her. It was all seriously awesome!

CHAPTER 18

Austen's older brother pulled up to Zoe's house, and Austen jumped out of the passenger side of the truck. "See you later, Ryan," he cried, slamming the door. "Tell Mom I'll ask Uncle Press for a ride home."

Just by luck, Austen and Ryan were passing through Katonah on their way back from Klumpie's Sports Equipment with Austen's new sneakers when he got Zoe's text: Brb in 30 with pup. Can u meet us?

When he didn't see Uncle Press's car in the driveway, he headed to the front porch steps to wait.

Getting a puppy is so cool, thought Austen, although he could barely remember when they got Kobe, their giant chocolate Lab, who was almost eight now. It was hard for him to imagine that huge one-hundred-pound bruiser as a puppy.

As the sun moved farther west, leafy oak trees started to shade the deep front porch. Austen brushed back the mop of blond curls from his face, stretched out his long legs, and relaxed. His day had gone by fast, but then, they always did when he was helping at the community garden. This morning was the first session of the compost workshop, and the staff had been surprised by how big the turnout was, so he had been busy.

Just hope I'm not too stinky, he thought, brushing off his cargo shorts again.

He'd stayed about an extra hour, but it was OK. His family's place, Horizon Farm in North Salem, was an easy bike ride to the garden. But the town center in Katonah was about eight miles away, too far by bike his mom said. Besides, the main roads were too busy.

Yesterday Olivia said that dude Ethan wanted to start this THREADS club, he thought. *That won't work for me if we always have to meet way down here in the village. Still, it sounds like it could be cool.*

It's funny how much time he'd been spending in Katonah's town center that summer, since Cousin Zoe and Aunt Camila had moved in along with Press. Before that, he didn't actually get to see too much of Zoe. She had lived so far away and had always been moving to different parts of Colorado. Now, when middle school started in September, he'd be seeing even more of Zoe— and her new friend Olivia.

A Jeep stopped at the curb and a girl about his age with super-long blond hair opened the front passenger door. "Wait here, Anna," she barked at the driver and then turned toward the house. Instantly, she stopped. One glimpse at Austen, with his golden curls, light-aqua T-shirt, and long tanned legs and, like a dimmer switch, her scowl became a big, bright smile.

"Oh, hi. I thought I left my lip gloss here," she said coming closer. "Is Zoe home?"

"No, they're all out," he answered.

She flicked a long, blond tress over her shoulder and said sweetly, "Really? Well, who are you?"

"Her cousin," replied Austen, thinking, *She's a little pushy.*

"OMG!" she said with a squeal. "Zoe told me about you. We were supposed to play tennis." Then Elin looked down. "OMG!" she cried again. "We have matching friendship bracelets. We're twins! Look!" She pointed to her ankle and his. They were both wearing a dark-blue, light-green, and orange Mega Diamond XXOO.

"Zoe gave me this," she gushed. "Is that how you got yours?"

The lady in the Jeep beeped impatiently and shouted out the window, "Elin, you come now. Your mother is waiting."

"Oh, that's just Anna, our au pair. Don't mind her," Elin said with a wave of her hand. "I'm Elin, that's spelled E-L-I-N," she told him.

Just then, Press's SUV turned into the driveway. They were back with the puppy! Austen jumped up and called out, "Hey, welcome home," and then ran over.

Elin looked surprised that he would just take off like that, but Anna started beeping again, so she got back into the Jeep and they drove away.

Press pulled the car to a very gentle stop, and then

Austen opened the door to the backseat. The sleepy pup was cuddled on Zoe's lap. "Wow! He is so little!" Austen said, leaning in. "Oh, hey. Hi, Olivia," he added.

"This is Carl," Zoe announced in an excited voice. "Say hello to your cousin Austen," she told the puppy.

"Carl! Great name!" Austen laughed. "Can I hold him?" He took Carl in his arms and said, "Hey, big buddy. Hello."

Zoe's mother looked over with a smile. "Why not take Carl into the backyard, Niña? It's fenced in, but keep him very close," she suggested. "We'll be with you in a minute. Press and I need to go over the shopping list."

Zoe and Olivia slowly walked to the backyard with Austen. Olivia noticed that he was not going to let go of the pup and smiled to herself. *Good with animals*, she thought. *Nice quality.*

When they were almost at the back gate, Zoe asked him, "Was that Elin Pierson out front?"

"Who?" Austen replied.

"Girl with long, blond hair?" she added, trying to get the gate latch open.

"Oh, yeah, that girl. I think that was her name, spelled E-L-I-N?"

Olivia smiled in relief. *Guess Austen wasn't another instant conquest for the most popular girl in fifth grade,* she thought. She reached out to help unlatch the gate, as it always gave people trouble, and they headed to the lawn area.

Back out in the driveway, Press was checking out the long list of puppy supplies. "Food, bowls, brush, leash, collar—this is like having a baby!"

Dr. Lopez laughed. "So true. Just remember you said you would get up when Carl wakes up in the middle of the night and has to go out to the yard."

Press laughed. "Oh, right. But, Camila, who was that girl with the very long hair talking to Austen when we drove up?"

"Elin Pierson. Remember I told you her mother owns the beauty salon, Magic Tresses? Maybe she'll be another new friend for Zoe," replied Dr. Lopez with a smile. "Although I wonder... I think Austen likes Olivia. The way they we're hanging out yesterday—"

"What?" interrupted Press. "Aren't they way too young for that?"

"Oh, honey, you have so much to learn," laughed Zoe's mom. "Now let's get going. Maybe Austen and Olivia can stay for dinner? That would be nice for Zoe."

"Hey, Uncle Press, can you give me a ride home later?" said Austen, coming around to the front. "My mom just texted."

"Sure," said Press, putting away the shopping list.

"And Zoe says don't forget the poop bags and the puppy wipes."

"OK, OK." He laughed. "Anything else?"

"Don't think so," said Austen and headed back to the yard, where Zoe and Olivia had put their feet together and created a little corral for Carl on the lawn.

Olivia was laughing, "Carl, Carl, let go of my hair. Let go." Carl had grabbed hold of her ponytail and was tugging on it.

"Yipes," said Austen. "I'll hold the ponytail. You hold the puppy," he said to Zoe.

Gently, they pulled the two apart. Austen couldn't

help noticing how silky Olivia's hair felt. *Carl, you're the man*, he thought.

CHAPTER 19

"Yuck! What is this I just stepped in?" cried Ethan. He raised his foot and frowned at the sole of his sneaker.

"I'm so sorry," said Zoe, reaching for the roll of paper towels. "We're trying to train Carl."

The first official meeting of THREADS was having a little trouble getting underway. Because of the puppy's arrival, all had agreed to relocate from Katonah Crafts and meet in Zoe's backyard instead.

"Come here, Carl," said Austen, squatting down. "I'll put him in his area over there, OK?" He lifted the puppy and put him down in the enclosure Press had made on the lawn with a low garden fence.

"And I'll sit here," said Zoe, pointing to a chair at the big, round patio table, "where I can keep my eye on him."

Underneath the large umbrella in the middle of the table, craft supplies and instruction sheets were spread out. Once Austen rejoined the group, they turned to Ethan.

"OK," he said, "here's the 411, which I think Olivia already told you. Maybe we can help some of the kids over in the Central Hospital with friendship bracelets. You know, bring them some or teach them how to do it? Olivia's mom has already given us flosses and instruction sheets to start."

Everyone nodded the same way they would have if they'd been listening to a teacher in school.

Zoe started looking through the instruction sheets. "So, Ethan, how does this actually work on the hospital side of things? I'm not clear on that," she asked, trying to understand the scope of the project.

Ethan was busy dividing the flosses into four equal piles.

"What do you mean?" he asked without looking up.

"I guess what I mean is, don't we have to get permission to go up to patients' rooms?" she replied. "We can't just walk in, right? Why don't we make a list of all the steps involved here, kind of like a game plan?"

When Ethan didn't reply, Austen said, "Once we figure out what all the steps are, we can decide who does what, right? I already spoke to my mom. She's in administration there, and she said we should meet with them once we come up with a plan."

Zoe nodded and said, "Yeah, and you know, I don't want to be a downer, but Press—that's my new father, Ethan—was asking last night if kids in the hospital spent a lot of time playing games, like electronic games on their phones. Are they really going to want to do this?"

"This is something else they can do," Olivia quickly pointed out, thinking, *THREADS is too good an idea to be dead on arrival.* "Seriously, they must need other activities," she added.

She reached into her new pink-and-gray-plaid backpack, the one that matched her new pink tank top with the fringe bottom. "I brought a notebook," she said while opening to page one and picking up her pen. She wrote "THREADS" on top of the page.

"So, Ethan, any ideas about how we should handle the hospital?" she asked.

Ethan didn't reply.

After a dead silence which didn't take long to become uncomfortable, Olivia realized that somehow they'd upset Ethan. She leaned over and asked him, "Are you OK? Is something wrong?"

"This was a stupid idea!" he blurted out. He stood up and pushed all the supplies in front of Olivia. "You keep this stuff. It's from Katonah Crafts anyway."

"Ethan, stop," said Olivia, feeling alarmed. "Don't be like that."

"Just forget it," he muttered and stormed out of the yard, slamming the gate behind him. Startled by the noise, Carl started to yip. Everyone else was too stunned to say anything.

Austen pushed back his chair and took off for the front. "Whoa, dude," he said, catching Ethan by the arm. "What's the problem?"

Ethan looked down. "Let go of me," he said.

"Seriously, what is your problem?" repeated Austen. "My mom will help us."

"I'm fine," Ethan said. "Just leave me alone."

Olivia felt awful. Ethan's meltdown was bad enough, but in front of Austen and Zoe? And Carl?

"Carl looks sleepy, doesn't he? Maybe he's going to take a nap," Zoe pointed out. "I'll put him in his crate inside. Maybe we should go down to Katonah Cupcakes?" She realized that a change of scene was needed, pronto. "Press is home. He'll look after him," she added.

Olivia was packing up the friendship bracelet supplies into the shopping bag from Katonah Crafts. "Sounds good," she agreed. "Can we drop these off at my mom's shop first?"

"Hey, we're not going to quit just because Ethan freaked out," Austen protested.

Oh no, served! Olivia's face turned as pink as her new top. *What was I thinking? What if Austen thinks I'm a quitter?* she thought.

"No, you're right. We're not going to quit. Zoe, can we keep the supplies here?"

The cupcake shop was a good idea. Olivia liked chocolate hazelnut, Zoe went for *tres leches*, and Austen said he was strictly a devil's food man. When they emerged with their treats, little kids and their parents and caregivers were taking up all the room on the outside benches, but the gazebo down by the train station was empty, so they headed there.

"This is cool," said Zoe, looking at the round table and circular bench inside the airy space.

"Kind of like school lunch," observed Austin, hoisting his long legs over the bench.

"Not in any of the schools I was in," laughed Zoe.

"How many have you been in?" Olivia asked, cutting her cupcake into neat quarters.

"This will be my fifth if you count preschool. But this will also be my last, besides high school," said Zoe. "Mama says so."

All three were quiet as they munched away at their treats. The most they could do was watch the traffic going down Main Street for a few minutes.

Olivia's father had long wanted to do something about that one-way street, she recalled. He always complained that there was usually some driver who made a wrong turn and caused a lot of commotion. That's kind of like

Ethan, Olivia realized, pleased with coming up with an image to illustrate his meltdown. He made the wrong turn and upset everybody.

"So, Olivia," said Austen after swallowing the last morsel of his cupcake, "what's the story with this Ethan dude? Has he always been weird?"

Olivia wished she had some milk. Her cupcake had way too much frosting, and her tongue felt glued to the top of her mouth. She started to cough and felt like a total klutz.

Finally, her throat was clear and she could talk. "Ethan kind of keeps to himself. But he's super smart. Maybe it was too much for him, being with other people? And we were asking him a lot of questions."

"I hope we didn't scare him off. I mean, the guy does have a great idea. Why don't we text him?" Austen suggested.

"Or send him a selfie? I have my phone," said Zoe, whipping it out. "Everybody put your heads together. Super, that looks super. Now what should we say?"

Austen had a suggestion. "How about, 'Knot for nothing, but we miss you'? Spelled *k-n-o-t*."

"That's cute," said Olivia, impressed that Austen was so nice. "Super. Send it, Zoe."

"OK, it's sent," she said, standing up. "But now I've got to get back to Carl."

"Right," replied Olivia. All three crossed the street. Olivia waved good-bye, and the two cousins walked up toward Bedford Road. She had a date to Skype with Alex at noon, but now, she had some extra time since the meeting of THREADS had flamed out.

Automatically, she headed down Main Street toward Katonah Crafts. The new clothing and accessory shop, Get Ups, was holding an early Fourth of July sale, and as she got closer, she could see they'd put bins of items on the sidewalk: scarves, flip-flops, tank tops, sunglasses. She tried on an oversize pair of glasses with leopard-print frames like Elin Pierson's and laughed at her reflection in the shop window. They were way too diva. But pretty soon, her thoughts started to wander back to THREADS. *What is bothering Ethan so much? Maybe I should ask Alex. She was always nice to him.* She tapped out a quick message, beginning with *"bracelet d'amitié"* knowing that the French for *friendship bracelet* would snag Alex's attention.

With a sad feeling, she realized that even though she and Alex had been in Village Elementary with Ethan since kindergarten, she really didn't known that much about him. Actually, she wasn't even really sure where he lived—probably in the village. He was always there on his skateboard. And he didn't seem to have too many friends either, 'cause if he had, why wouldn't he have asked them to be in THREADS?

The door to Magic Tresses swung open, and Elin Pierson herself came flying out looking seriously ticked off. She disappeared next door into Katonah Beans, and faster than an instant message, Olivia hightailed it down the block to Katonah Crafts.

The late morning light was super bright and sunny, and the outer door was open. It took a few moments for Olivia's eyes to adjust to the darker interior, but once they did, she could see someone was seated at the crafts table—a tallish, dark-haired someone, like Ethan Fleckman. And he was working on a friendship bracelet.

Quickly, she turned her eyes toward the front counter, where Miss Ruth Ann was scanning the computer, probably tracking the inventory. "Good morning, Miss Ruth Ann," she said. "How are you?"

"Why, good morning, Olivia," Miss Ruth Ann replied. "I'm fine, thank you so much." She gestured toward the crafts table. "Your friend Ethan popped in bright and early."

Olivia nodded and was instantly worried. *Will Ethan pitch a fit in here too? In front of Zoe and Austen was bad enough, but that can't possibly happen in front of Miss Ruth Ann.*

Telling herself to stay calm, she approached the crafts table. When Ethan said nothing, she pulled out a chair and sat down.

"Hi, Ethan," she said in her gentle voice. "Can I see what you're making?"

He didn't even look at her but stopped working and slid his unfinished project her way. In big letters was woven *THREA*.

Olivia couldn't believe it. "This is amazing!" she exclaimed. "You're spelling out *THREADS*?"

"Yeah," he muttered.

Miss Ruth Ann had walked over, and she leaned down to check out the project as well. She nodded in approval, saying, "Ethan is so clever."

"Yes, he is," Olivia said.

When Ethan didn't reply, Olivia kicked his leg under the table and made a tiny nod toward Miss Ruth Ann.

He took the hint. "Thank you, Miss Ruth Ann," he said.

Olivia thought, *Mom's rule number one in Katonah Crafts has always been to be nice to Miss Ruth Ann. Since Ethan practically lives here, he better obey it.*

"So does mean that you still want to do it? I mean, still want to have THREADS?" she whispered, almost afraid of the answer.

"Yeah…I guess so."

"Super!" said Olivia, relieved. "I'll text Zoe."

"No. I will."

"OK," Olivia said with a shrug.

Miss Ruth Ann was heading toward the big supply room off the rear of the main shopping area. "Olivia, would you help me for a minute?" she called out.

"Sure," Olivia said, pushing back her chair.

"You're getting nice and tall," Miss Ruth Ann said to Olivia while closing the supply room door. "Can you reach that ream of printing paper up there on the middle shelf?"

Olivia took down the paper and handed it over.

"Thank you so much," said Miss Ruth Ann. "Your mother told me about THREADS. Anything I can do to help, I will. You do know I volunteer at the hospital and can help you make contacts there?"

"You can?" Olivia said. "That's wonderful. I'll tell Ethan." She reached for the doorknob.

"Just a second, Olivia. I hope you keep in mind that Ethan seems to be a loner, or maybe he's just lonely. Many creative people are. Don't lose patience with him."

"I won't, Miss Ruth Ann. But that's super good news about the hospital." Olivia couldn't wait to tell Ethan. She hurried back into the front of the shop, but the crafts table was empty.

Ethan was gone.

CHAPTER 20

Four days later, the club met again in Zoe's backyard. Everyone was knocked out when Ethan surprised them with friendship bracelets. "Thought we could wear these at the hospital," he said, handing a bracelet to Zoe, Olivia, and then Austen.

They were identical: brown and orange with the word *THREADS* woven in the middle. Olivia was astounded, first by the bracelet and then by how he'd gotten so much done. *He's like a machine*, she thought in awe.

"I put a blue bead on yours, Olivia, for loyalty. Zoe's is yellow for happy, and Austen's is brown, for confidence," he explained.

"Why is your bead black?" Zoe asked.

"Uh, that's for smart," Ethan replied with a little blush.

"Oh, really?" laughed Zoe.

"That's cool. Thanks, buddy," Austen told him with a pat on the back. "Tie mine on, Zoe?"

After all four members tied theirs on and were completely official, Ethan reached into his backpack.

"And here's a bigger one for Carl," he said. "He'll only be able to wear it for a while before he grows too much."

The wide band said *THREADS CARL*.

"Oh, Ethan, this is so super!" cried Zoe.

"Yeah!" said Austen, lifting up the pup to tie it on.

"Seriously," agreed Olivia.

"I can make a bigger one for your dog, Sullivan," Ethan told her.

He is really getting into this, thought Olivia. "Super. I'll measure his neck and text you, OK?"

Ethan nodded in agreement and then said, "So Miss Ruth Ann said she can help us at the hospital."

"And my mom can help us too," Austin added.

Zoe was used to teamwork from being in sports. "Why don't we start by making some samples? You know, easy for beginners, medium, and advanced?" she suggested.

"I'll do a few of the easy ones," Austen laughed.

"And I'll help you," Zoe piped up. "Maybe I'll do a medium too?"

"I'll do the advanced," offered Ethan.

"Great!" said Zoe. "What do you want to do, Olivia?"

Olivia surprised herself by blurting out, "I'll make a flyer about THREADS. We can use it to meet with the hospital."

"Great idea, Olivia," Austen agreed right away.

"So let's get to work and meet back here in a few days," Zoe said. "I'll text everyone?"

With nothing else to discuss, they all stood up and got ready to leave. "Zoe, do you still have the supplies?" Ethan asked, looking around.

"Yep. I brought out the bag before," said Zoe, reaching down beside her chair and plopping it on the table. Only now it wasn't what she expected. The supply bag was in shreds.

Immediately, all four members leaned down and looked under the table. Carl was chomping away with flosses tangled all over his teeth and paws.

"OMG!" Zoe cried. "Carl! Carl!"

"That's about as guilty as they come." Austen laughed.

Ethan slumped back into a chair and sat there, just staring at the soggy heap that was their supplies.

"It's not that bad," Olivia said, quickly springing to the puppy's defense. She started sorting out the dry ones from the wet, but there was too much damage. Soon, she had to give up.

"Let's go down to Katonah Crafts and pick out some new ones," she suggested. "Mom will understand."

"I'm so sorry, everyone," said Zoe, trying to untangle Carl from the big mess.

"Oh, puppies are like that," Austen pointed out.

Ethan stood up. "Yeah, right," he said.

The meeting was over.

CHAPTER 21

"*Mais oui.* Yep, so Ethan got over his meltdown and THREADS is back on track," Olivia was telling Alex on Skype.

"Wonder what made Ethan freak out like that?"

Olivia shrugged. "Maybe he's moody, *tu'sais*? You know?"

Alex laughed and said, "Oh, Ollie, I meant to tell you that you look really good. I like your hair in that long braid. Turn around. Is it a French braid?"

"Yes! Camp Monroe starts this morning, remember?"

"Cool! Hey, say hello to Mu Mu for me and send me a pic. I want to see her new braces, *ses bagues*."

"OK. Not sure she has *ses bagues* yet, but will do. Are you going to see Fabien?"

"Yes! He's in my French class later this afternoon. His family just moved here from Vermont, so his mom wants his French to be perfect. Oh, Ollie, my screen is cutting out..."

"Love you!" cried Olivia, turning off the connection and heading toward the kitchen.

Since it was time to get ready for camp, she reached for the peanut butter and jelly to make a sandwich when her dad came in with Sullivan from their walk.

"OK, Ollie, do you have everything you need?" he asked.

"Yes, Dad. I've done this before, remember?"

Her father opened the pantry door and took out a fruit and nut bar. "Take this just in case you get hungry," he said.

"Dad, this isn't preschool," she laughed, stashing it in her backpack.

Olivia and Alex had always loved camp. They had gone there since kindergarten. In fact, that's where they first met and became instant BFFs.

OK, so things have changed. At least Mu Mu will be

there, she reminded herself as she headed out the side door. The morning was sunny and the air felt fresh. *Like seashore Nantucket fresh*, Olivia thought, remembering the beach cottage they had all gone to for a week every August. But no Alex this summer. That was going to seem weird. With a swift motion, she threw back the kickstand on her bike and took off for the short ride to Monroe Park.

When she arrived, the place was first-day crazy, swarming with parents and kids trying to find their groups. Olivia almost knocked over two little boys who bumped into her as they screamed and horsed around. *They're probably in the five/sixes*, she thought. As she elbowed her way over to the picnic area where the counselors usually set up their tables, she noticed that most of the campers were way younger than she was. Maybe it was a good thing that this was her last year there. Was she outgrowing camp?

But over by the snack bar, there was a familiar face. It was Mu Mu. *Whew!*

Mu Mu spotted her too and waved. "Hey, hey!" she

shouted, threading her way over. She planted herself right in front of Olivia and turned on a huge smile.

All Olivia could do was stare.

Spanning Mu Mu's top and bottom teeth were bright-pink-and-green braces. "Well, what's the verdict?" she asked.

"Amazing!" replied Olivia, thinking, *That is so bold!*

"Go big or go home, right?" said Mu Mu with a loud laugh.

"Right!" said Olivia, who couldn't help laughing too.

"But you don't you think they look too preppy?" Mu Mu asked with concern.

"Oh, no," Olivia said, shaking her head.

A shrill whistle cut off their conversation. "Eleven/twelve girls! Eleven/twelve girls! Go to table six!" a counselor shouted into a bullhorn.

Olivia and Mu Mu found their table, and soon, a small group started to form around them.

A woman in her early twenties wearing a T-shirt and a whistle on a lanyard loudly clapped her hands. "OK, girls. I'm Ashley, and I'll be your counselor." And then she pointed to a young teenager beside her. "And this is Parker, your counselor-in-training or CIT. OK?"

"Hi, everybody," said Parker with a tiny wave.

"We've made up name tags for today, so we can learn who's who," said Ashley. CIT Parker started walking around and giving each camper a tag.

Olivia checked out the group. There was no one she knew from Village Elementary or flute lessons or anywhere else. As her eyes roamed, she noticed a couple of girls giggling and pointing at her. Mu Mu noticed too. "Hey, your name tag is on upside down," she whispered.

Quickly, Olivia pulled it off and put it back the right way.

"OK, quiet. Quiet, everybody," shouted Ashley. "I have two leftover tags. Where is Kennedy Washington and where is Elin Pierson? That's spelled *E-L-I-N*?"

Ouch! Olivia closed her eyes and thought, *I didn't see that coming. Elin has never been in camp before.*

"Here, we're right here," said Elin, strolling over with Kennedy. She was wearing her leopard-print sunglasses and carrying a hot-pink fringe bag over her shoulder.

"OK, girls," said Ashley, handing them their name tags. "Can you try to be on time from now on?"

"Sorry," said Elin in a breezy voice. "The au pair was running late again."

Mu Mu rolled her eyes. "Check out that diva," she whispered to Olivia.

"Olivia Jones, Mu Mu Lin, Elin, and Kennedy, you're Team Unicorn," shouted Parker. "Can you stand together?" Olivia and Mu Mu shot each other looks and laughed.

A few minutes later, Team Unicorn was sitting under a tall oak waiting for Parker to finish putting all the groups together.

"Let me show you my new selfies," Elin said to Kennedy as she reached into her fringed bag for her phone. "Here's me with Zoe's new puppy, Carl."

She held up her phone and showed Kennedy the photo. "Cute!" Kennedy gushed. "I love your new earrings!"

"Oh, and here's me with Austen. He's so hot!" Elin continued.

"Oh, yeah, super hot. Sooo stellar!" Kennedy squealed, giving her buddy a high five.

"Maybe I'll see him later for Frappuccino," Elin said, checking her texts.

Olivia wanted to die. Right there, right then.

"Which Austen are you talking about?" said Mu Mu, reaching out for Elin's phone and flicking through the photos. "Oh, yeah, I know him. It's Austen Dodd. We were at Meadowlark Elementary together. Yeah, he's super popular."

Austen and Elin—Mr. Super Popular and Miss Super Popular, thought Olivia, looking down at the ground. *Makes sense.*

A young camper running their way interrupted her funk. "Who's Olivia?" she asked breathlessly. Olivia raised her hand. "Ashley wants to see you," the camper said, trying to make her errand sound important, "over at table six. Right away."

Olivia shrugged.

"Don't worry," Mu Mu said with a laugh. "You can't be in trouble. It's way too soon. We just got here."

Olivia laughed too. "Be right back," she said and then made her way to the picnic table, where her counselor was talking on the phone.

"OK, I'll ask her," Ashley said. "Yeah, yeah, I'll text you." She clicked off, looked at Olivia, and explained, "The five/sixes' arts and crafts instructor couldn't make it. Can you fill in and show them how to make some simple friendship bracelets, like that blue-and-white one you're wearing? Your mother owns the crafts store, right? We figured you would know your way around stuff like that."

"Sure," replied Olivia. "Do you want me to go now?"

"If you could. Start with table two, over there by the water fountain. Heather, the camp director, will meet you there. Thanks!"

"I'll just get my backpack," Olivia said, pointing in the direction of Team Unicorn. Running back, she was so distracted by the idea of getting away from Elin that she twisted her ankle stepping on an acorn and had to hop the rest of the way to the tall oak tree.

When she heard the news, Mu Mu was definitely not a happy camper. "You're ditching me?" she wailed dramatically and loud enough for both Elin and Kennedy to hear.

Olivia tried to soften the blow and quietly said, "It's just temporary. I'll see you at lunch, OK?"

"No! I'm coming with you," said Mu Mu, jumping to her feet. "I'll be your assistant. See you, Elin. See you, Kennedy."

CHAPTER 22

"My mom told me there's an old saying that if you wear a friendship bracelet until it falls off, your wish will come true," said Mu Mu. "Is that true, Miss Ruth Ann?"

"Well, I can't be sure that your wish will come true, Mu Mu, but yes, there is an old saying that goes like that. Or maybe your bracelet falls off after your wish comes true? Look up there," said the shop's manager, pointing to the two very same mottoes hanging in a frame above the embroidery floss section.

Olivia had to smile. Who would have thought bold, funny Mu Mu and the very proper Miss Ruth Ann would become BFFs so fast? But when Olivia and her new friend had made their way into Katonah Crafts after camp, it had taken only a nanosecond for Mu Mu to feel right at home.

"I've only been in here once or twice," explained Mu Mu. "Since we live close to Ridgefield, you know, right over the border in Connecticut, we usually go there. I don't remember ever meeting you, Miss Ruth Ann."

"And I am sure I would remember you, Mu Mu," replied Miss Ruth Ann with a smile.

Earlier in the day, the girls' time as substitute arts and crafts instructors at camp went well, so well that Olivia and Mu Mu were asked to stay on as instructors for the entire week. For one thing, Mu Mu turned out to be a whiz at explaining how to make friendship bracelets. And for another, she soon had the campers laughing.

"Looks like you've got them in stitches," Olivia had joked, super pleased by how her morning had been snatched from the jaws of disaster. Or at least that was how it had felt at the time.

One little boy camper, Aiden Sanchez, who had picked up the weaving fast, told them his older sister said the colors had meanings. "Yes, they do," Olivia had replied. "Would you like to know what they are?"

Aiden nodded his head up and down.

"OK, well, tomorrow, we'll tell you what they all mean," she said, looking at Mu Mu, who gave her a thumbs-up.

After the last of their morning sessions, Olivia had suggested that she and Mu Mu visit Katonah Crafts and note down Miss Ruth Ann's chart of colors. Olivia was going to take a copy of it to camp the next morning.

They were lucky the shop was quiet. Only a few little girls were over by the bead bins with their mothers, so Mu Mu and Olivia had the entire crafts table to themselves. "Light blue is for loyalty, right?" said Mu Mu, pointing to Olivia's bracelet. "And white is for peace?"

"That's right," replied Olivia, almost done copying Miss Ruth Ann's chart. There was plenty of foam-core poster board at home, so Olivia decided that later that night, she'd get out her markers and make her own chart. Hmm... Maybe she'd also make up smaller charts and print out one for each camper.

Mu Mu thought that was a super idea. "Aiden will love it. He can show his sister," she pointed out. "You know how kids love to have something to show off."

"Really?" said Olivia, copying down that lime green equaled lucky and orange stood for energetic. "Then I'll bring my markers, and maybe we can write the name of each camper on their chart?"

"Super idea!" shouted Mu Mu, giving her a high five. "You're on fire. Team Unicorn, watch out! We may never be back!"

Olivia started to laugh. "Team Who-nicorn?" she joked.

"Wow!" laughed Mu Mu, giving her a double high five. "Outstanding!"

Drawn by their laughter, Miss Ruth Ann started walking their way. "Oh, Olivia, I have some flosses for Ethan. I haven't seen him today," she said.

"Who's Ethan?" Mu Mu piped up.

Olivia finished writing that black stands for smart and then folded up her colors list. "Oh, he's a kid in my class, or was in my class at Village Elementary. He comes in here a lot," she told her in a low voice, the kind of voice that means "no questions." But she did add, "He'll be in middle school in September too."

Miss Ruth Ann looked at Olivia for a long moment and seemed as though she was about to say something, but instead she walked over to the bead bins to help the young girls.

Right away, Olivia worried. *Hope Miss Ruth Ann doesn't think I wasn't being loyal to Ethan. But if I tell Mu Mu about THREADS, she might ask to be in the club. And if I invite someone else, Ethan could freak out again.*

Being torn like that between people was definitely not a good feeling. Now she knew what her dad meant when he talked about being between a rock and a hard place. But unfortunately for Olivia, her downer spell was quickly replaced by another dilemma. The doorbell to Katonah Crafts jingled, and in walked Elin Pierson with Kennedy Washington. Both were carrying plastic cups that said *FRAPPE, FRAPPE, FRAPPE* on the outside.

Instantly, Olivia's alarms began to go off: *Uh-oh, when Miss Ruth Ann sees they brought drinks in here, she's going to come down on them like...like what?* She took a few seconds to think of the perfect image. *Not like a ton of bricks. Everybody says that. Yes! I've got it: like a 9.5 magnitude earthquake, the largest one in history, the one we studied in science. Hmm…maybe that's over the top, but still, maybe I should warn them?*

"Hey, Team Unicorn!" Mu Mu loudly greeted the girls.

Elin lowered her sunglasses as if she didn't recognize them and said, "Oh, hi."

Mu Mu laughed and turned to Olivia. "All finished?" she asked.

"Yup," replied Olivia, nodding toward the front door. Then, in what she hoped was her nicest voice, she said, "Oh, Kennedy and Elin, there's no food allowed in here," and pointed to a sign at the counter.

"Whatever," said Elin.

"Seriously?" Olivia shot back.

Elin stared at her. Miss Ruth Ann's head jerked up, and she seemed as if she were about to fly over. *Kind of like the way a cannonball flies from a cannon*, Olivia thought.

Olivia held out her hands. "I can put your drinks by the front door for you," she offered.

Elin rolled her eyes, but both she and Kennedy gave Olivia their cups.

"They're empty!" Olivia said in surprise.

Elin just smirked.

Outside, Olivia noticed the litter basket was overflowing, so she tossed the cups in the next one she saw, next to Magic Tresses. And then a great idea hit her. "Mu Mu, it's still pretty early. Want to come back to my house? We could make brownies before your mom has to get you."

"No nuts?" asked Mu Mu, pointing to her braces.

"No nuts," laughed Olivia. "Extra chocolate!"

"I have a new recipe that sounds super. Want to try it? Believe it or not, it has black pepper in it."

"Super," said Olivia.

Tomorrow after camp, she was going to Dr. Justin's office herself for her new blue-and-white braces. She decided she might as well start to live without nuts now.

CHAPTER 23

The warm, chocolaty aroma of brownies filled Olivia with joy. What was it like, she asked herself, trying to find a poetic image. Was it like the scent of hyacinths on the first warm spring day? Or maybe, it was like new conditioner she had used that morning, "Sea Salt Spray," that reminded her of Surfside Beach in Nantucket?

Mu Mu had picked up on the scent too and stared at the oven with a brightness in her eyes. When the timer went off, Olivia set the baking pan on a rack to cool, but before she could even get out a cake plate, the front doorbell rang. "Be right back," she promised and rushed to the front entrance, where Sullivan was barking wildly.

"Now, don't jump," Olivia warned him, opening the door.

Austen was standing there, and behind him on the steps was Ethan. Immediately, Sullivan jumped all over him.

Wow! What brought these two here? she thought, pulling the dog away.

"Hey, Olivia, look who came to visit," said Austen, pointing to the end of the front garden, where Zoe was hovering over Carl, who was busy sniffing the oregano and thyme Olivia's mom planted last month. Zoe looked so happy and proud.

"Mu Mu, come here!" yelled Olivia. "You have to see this."

Really? thought Mu Mu and reluctantly tore herself away from the brownies and headed outside.

"Oh!" she gasped when she saw the puppy. Immediately, she plunked down on the walkway and opened her arms. Carl pulled on his leash and scampered over, wagging his tail like they were old BFFs. With a laugh, Mu Mu lifted him up and buried her face in his soft fur, crying over and over, "Carl! Carl!"

"Guess everyone loves a puppy," said Zoe, watching with a grin.

"Hey, do I smell brownies?" Ethan abruptly asked, pointing to the open front door.

"Oh, right. They're just out of the oven," said Olivia. "I'll get some."

Sullivan was so in love with his puppy brother he hadn't even bothered to pester them for some of the rich, peppery brownies, which dogs can't have anyway, Olivia explained, because chocolate could be toxic to them.

But that didn't stop Ethan and Austen from joining the empty-plate club. Now they were sprawled out on the porch steps. "So, Mu Mu, do you think these Katonah kids can keep up with us at middle school?" Austen asked his old classmate.

Mu Mu laughed. "No way! Meadowlark is way harder than Village Elementary"

"Says who?" challenged Ethan.

From the round table on the porch where she'd been sitting with Carl cuddled on her lap, Zoe watched the back and forth with growing interest. "Oh, so that's how it is? You guys from different elementary schools compete?"

"Yep, well, maybe at first. But don't forget there are all those kids from Titicus Elementary too," Austen pointed out. "It's a big middle school, three elementary schools going into one huge sixth grade."

"Hey, Ethan, where did you get that skateboard?" Mu Mu suddenly asked. "I like your purple wheels and camo grip tape."

"Uh, I made it," he replied.

"Wow! Really? Can I take it for a ride?" she asked, pushing back her chair and jumping down the steps.

For a few moments, Ethan looked as if he were about to say no. But instead, he nodded. "OK."

With her right foot on the deck, Mu Mu pushed off and then, crouching down, made the tight turn onto the front sidewalk and zoomed out of sight toward Bedford Road. After a couple of minutes, she sailed back. Without missing a beat, she jumped off in front of Ethan, kicked the board up, and handed it to him.

"Sweet," she said. "Thanks."

Olivia's eyes widened. Mu Mu was full of surprises.

She thought, *We definitely need her in THREADS. She's not afraid to ask for what she wants.*

"Hey, did I tell you guys that Mu Mu and I taught arts and crafts at Camp Monroe this morning?"

"Really?" said Zoe. Ethan looked up and Olivia made eye contact with him. "Yep. And Mu Mu is super good at making friendship bracelets," she continued.

Mu Mu laughed. "Hey, it was either that or be in Team Unicorn by myself. But it was fun, right, Olivia? We showed the campers how to do simple patterns with two colors, like Olivia's blue-and-white one," she said, pointing at Olivia's bracelet.

"Cool," said Ethan and then stood up. He threw his skateboard on the front walk. "Gotta go. See you guys." Then he pushed off and rolled away.

Bummer, thought Olivia. *Guess Ethan wasn't going to act on my hint about Mu Mu and the friendship bracelets. She would be lots of fun in THREADS.*

Mu Mu watched him and turned to Olivia. "Was it something I said?" she asked with a laugh.

"Oh, no," Olivia hastened to reassure her. "That's just Ethan and his weird ways."

"We should go too, Carl," said Zoe, picking up her puppy. "Press said not to keep him out too long."

"Bye, bye, Carl," said Mu Mu, giving him a kiss.

"See you, see you," Olivia said, waving as the cousins walked away. Fresh from his nap, Carl was yanking his leash every which way.

When they disappeared from sight, Mu Mu took a deep breath and said, "Your friends are cool, Olivia." Then she checked her phone and added, "It's almost five. My mom will be here any minute. I'll run inside and get my backpack, OK? We have to pick up my brother from swim practice."

Olivia hunkered down on the stoop with Sullivan. When Mu Mu returned, Olivia told her, "I'll make the color charts tonight."

"OK," Mu Mu said and then glanced down the road, watching for her mother's SUV. In a very different voice, a serious voice, she added, "Olivia, please don't mention Zoe's puppy to my mom, OK?"

"Zoe's puppy?" replied Olivia, confused.

"Please, just don't mention Carl," repeated Mu Mu.

Olivia nodded. "I won't. Promise. But I don't get it," she started saying.

"A little while ago, Zoe told me that Carl came from Golden's Bridge. Was the breeder Mrs. Mumford?"

"Um, yes."

Mu Mu blinked and appeared as though she was trying to decide something. Then she faced Olivia and said in a soft voice, "We went there too. Carl was supposed to be ours, but at the last minute…uh, something happened. And Mom was really, really upset. We had gone to visit him every week since he was born."

Immediately, Olivia felt terrible. *OMG! Mu Mu's family was the last-minute cancellation Mrs. Mumford mentioned? That's why Carl jumped all over her like they were BFFs!*

"I'm so sorry! I'm so sorry! I had no idea!" Olivia cried. "That had to be so hard for you. Oh, and Elin and her stupid selfies too!"

Mu Mu just shook her head, like she was toughing it

out. "Look, I don't want any pity parties. Besides, Mom says there will be other dogs. I just…I just didn't want you to bring it up 'cause then she'll feel bad again. So please don't tell Zoe…or anyone. Oh, here's Mom now. See you tomorrow!" she said, running toward the car.

Olivia held on to Sullivan's collar so he wouldn't chase after Mu Mu, and then as the car disappeared from sight, she sank down onto the front porch steps. Wrapping her arms around the dog's big, furry neck, she whispered, "Sully, I am so lucky to have you."

I'll never tell anyone about Carl, she thought, *not even Alex. Mu Mu is so strong. I'm not sure I could do that…*

Her phone started to beep. She looked down to find a text from Ethan. Can u ask Mu Mu 2 b in threads?

OK, she texted back right away. Only now she was not exactly sure Mu Mu would want to.

CHAPTER 24

Brown is confident, light purple is beautiful, and yellow is happy.

Well, thought Olivia, picking up the mirror to examine her blue-and-white braces again. *Confident, beautiful, and happy, that wouldn't be bad. Tomorrow after camp, I'll get some embroidery flosses and make myself a really big brown, purple, and yellow wristband, one that will last a whole year, or at least as long as I have to wear these braces.*

"Ollie, come. Come downstairs," Olivia's dad called from the foot of the stairs. "Time for dinner."

What will this be like? Olivia thought, heading down with Sullivan at her heels. *Will Mom and Dad give me lots of pep talks? Or will Dad keep singing, "Embrace me, my sweet embraceable you"? Mom says he's just being sweet... but wow!*

Much to her surprise, dinner went by in a kind of a normal way, and her mom made Olivia's favorite pasta, linguine with clam sauce, which Olivia and Alex had fallen in love with in Nantucket long ago, except that night, her mom chopped up the clams into tiny, tiny pieces.

Later, as Olivia snuggled into bed with Sullivan resting on the floor in his cozy dog couch, she knew that the next day would be her big test. But big as that was, she couldn't shake thoughts of Mu Mu and the puppy and of Zoe and all the times she and her mom had to move. With her eyelids growing heavy, she realized, *They faced way bigger hurdles than new braces and didn't choke. I won't either.*

She leaned over the edge of the bed and said, "Right, Sully? Right, Sully?"

His belly was rising up and down as he snored away with his mouth open and his tongue hanging out the side. "Sully is lucky," she said to herself in a drowsy voice. "His teeth look perfect…but what if he had a crossbite? A dog with braces, blue-and-white braces… That's silly. Silly Sully…"

CHAPTER 25

Skype service was out only temporarily, but it was long enough that Olivia had to leave for Camp Monroe before showing her BFF the new braces. She was really hoping to get a boost from Alex, a "they look cool" pat on the back. *Well, I'll just have to handle the reaction*, she thought, riding up the hill toward the park.

At camp, nobody even noticed. Or at least, no one said anything, except for Mu Mu, who screamed out, "They're so cute!" The rest of Team Unicorn, Elin and Kennedy, were nowhere to be seen.

Olivia was almost disappointed—she'd built the braces thing up so much in her head. But soon she told herself that flying below the radar was a good thing, and her mood improved.

At snack break, Mu Mu was totally her old self, making jokes and giving out tips, especially about which Chinese foods were OK for braces.

"Wonton soups, OK. Spareribs, uh-uh. Spring rolls, they're a definite maybe, depending where you get them," she pointed out. "The ones at Golden Panda don't have a lot of sticky things."

Olivia nodded and thought, *Mu Mu is in a good mood. Maybe now would be a good time to mention THREADS?*

"So, let me tell you about this great idea Ethan just came up with," she started saying.

"Ethan Fleckman, you mean?" asked Mu Mu, taking out a mirror from her backpack to check that her braces were clean.

"Yup, Ethan Fleckman," Olivia continued and then sketched out the idea.

Mu Mu seemed interested, and Olivia made a big point of mentioning Ethan's text. "Sounds cool," she said. "Who else is in it? Just Austen and Zoe and you?"

"Right," replied Olivia.

"Sure. When is the next meeting?"

"Friday afternoon. Is that OK?" And then, trying to be totally up front about the puppy, Olivia added, "But, Mu Mu, we're probably going to meet at Zoe's because she doesn't want to leave Carl yet. Is that OK too?"

"Yeah, yeah, why not? I'll make a couple of bracelets. Do you have Ethan's phone number? I'll text him," Mu Mu casually replied and then asked, "Hey, Olivia, BTW, did you see Elin and Kennedy this morning after roll call?"

"Nope."

"Me either. Do you think they dropped out? Will Team Unicorn be down by two?" she joked.

Olivia shrugged. "Maybe."

Their conversation was cut short. Ashley the counselor started clapping her hands. "OK, everybody, listen up. Elin Pierson and Kennedy Washington won't be here for a few days. Now I want you all to pay strict attention. In case you don't know, this is a photo of a poison ivy plant," she started explaining to the campers.

Parker, the counselor-in-training, walked around the group holding up the photo for everyone to see.

Ashley continued. "Before you step into the woods or anywhere there is undergrowth, watch where you are walking. Avoid this plant or, to be safe, any plant with three leaves. Teach yourself, 'Leaves of three, let it be.' Let's all say that: leaves of three, let it be. OK, good. Remember, poison ivy is a vine, and it also can climb up trees or wind itself around shrubs. Any questions?"

Nobody said anything for a few moments. Then Mu Mu asked, "So, is this why Elin and Kennedy aren't here? Did they get poison ivy?"

"I really can't discuss other campers," Ashley replied, "but let's say I want all you girls to be safe rather than sorry."

"Gross!" whispered Mu Mu to Olivia. "Have you ever had poison ivy? It's the worst! I did last summer, and I itched for weeks. It was so bad I didn't even want to think about food."

"Wow! That's really bad," Olivia whispered back. "I've had it too. It's super yucky!"

CHAPTER 26

"OK, everybody," Ethan started saying. "Let's see what you've got."

Friday turned out to be rainy, so camp was canceled and the afternoon meeting of THREADS at Zoe's was moved indoors. A few minutes earlier, she had arranged chairs around the bamboo table in the long, screened-in back porch and set Carl's crate next to her chair.

Ethan and Austen were the first to arrive and immediately attacked the bowl of tortilla chips and salsa Zoe had put out on a nearby coffee table.

When Olivia rang the front doorbell, she was trying to stay focused on THREADS. But it was the first time she had actually been back inside her old BFF's place since

Zoe had moved in. She was OK when she went through the family room and kitchen, places where she and Alex had spent countless hours, but when she got close to the porch, her eyes immediately went to the doorframe. *Oh!* she thought. *It's still there.*

On the left side was the growth chart where Alex and her brothers, and Olivia too, had their heights measured and recorded. Stopping to look, Olivia was amazed. *Can it be that the last entry was only two months ago?*

Zoe noticed how distracted Olivia was. "You know what? Let's add my name and Carl's? Look, here's a pencil and a tape measure," she said, reaching over to her supplies on the table. "I'll get Carl out of his crate. Can you measure us?"

"Sure, that's a great idea," said Olivia, making a mark on the frame between her height and Alex's. *Can this be right? Zoe is only two inches shorter than me?* She was surprised. She thought Zoe was a lot shorter.

When they were done, Zoe asked, "So, do you like these bracelets I made?" She pushed up the sleeve on her sky-blue top and held out her arm.

"Wow! Super," said Olivia looking down at four bracelets, all done in different patterns.

Zoe pointed to each bracelet. "This blue-and-gray one is fishtail braid. This is heart. This pink, black, and white one is diamond, and then I made this chain stitch with a button."

Ethan was sitting at the round table unpacking his shark backpack. "A button? Let me see, Zoe."

"OK. Here, you hold Carl," she said, plopping the puppy in his lap. Ethan seemed flustered when Carl started licking his face, but Zoe just laughed. She was busy showing him her bracelets when Mu Mu burst in.

"Hello, THREADS!" she shouted from the doorway, brushing the raindrops off her orange tank top. "Your dad let me in, Zoe. Sorry I'm late. Heavy rain out on Route 35. How did you get here, Austen?"

"Rowboat," he joked. "No, seriously, my brother, Ryan, dropped me off earlier. Yeah, it's really bad out there!"

"Sure is, so check out my bracelets," she said, digging into her pink-and-black backpack. She took out a plastic baggie, slid open the zipper, and put a handful of bracelets on the table. "Here's watermelon slices, candy corn, pretzel, and chocolate chip."

Olivia had to laugh, but only to herself. All of Mu Mu's patterns were about food. *The braces must be driving her crazy*, she thought.

"Mu Mu, these are really amazing," she said, handing them around so the other members could see.

Ethan examined each one carefully. "Yeah, they are. So, uh, here's something for you." He slid over a THREADS bracelet.

"Wow! This is super! This is mine? Wait, all of you have them? OMG!" Mu Mu said, checking out the other members'. "Wait, why do I have an orange bead?"

"Uh, that's for energetic," answered Ethan.

"OK, I'll take that," said Mu Mu with a laugh. "Tie it on for me?"

Ethan made a strong knot and then started drumming his fingers on the table. "So, Austen, how did you do with your projects?"

Austen appeared a little shy. Actually, Olivia thought he looked adorable.

"Hey, OK, nobody laugh," said Austen, reaching into his khaki backpack for three bracelets, all done in a simple arrow pattern, just like the blue-and-white one Olivia's mom had given her. No one made a comment. "You said to do easy, right?" he asked.

"It's important to have a range," pointed out Olivia, rising to his defense. "So what do you guys think of these charts I made up?" she asked, handing everyone a What Colors Stand For chart, like those she and Mu Mu had given out at camp.

"And here's the THREADS flyer," she added, passing around copies. "If it's OK, maybe Austen can show it to his mother? And then we can find out what the next step is? Don't forget, Miss Ruth Ann at Katonah Crafts said she would help us too. I told you she volunteers at the hospital."

Quiet filled the sunporch while they checked out Olivia's materials.

Ethan finished first and said, "Sounds like you covered everything. We'll make bracelets for the kids, or they can choose from what we already have made up, or we'll come to the hospital and work with them."

"Yeah, Olivia, good job," Austen said. "OK, everybody? OK to show my mom?"

They all nodded. Ethan packed up the bracelets in small plastic bags according to level of difficulty, adding his own samples to the advanced group, and handed them to Austen.

"So after I show everything to my mom, I'll text you all, OK?" Austen said.

"Here are a few extra copies of the flyer," said Olivia, sliding a folder to Austen along with a big plastic baggie for all the smaller baggies of the bracelet samples. He carefully placed everything in his backpack and zipped it closed.

"Anything else?" he asked.

Before anyone could reply, the front doorbell rang. Three times, right in a row. "Who's that?" said Zoe.

Carl started to bark, and it was such a loud bark for a little puppy that they all started to laugh.

"Good dog, Carl, good watchdog," Zoe said, scooping him up and heading to the front door. "I'll be right back."

When she returned a few minutes later, Elin Pierson

and Kennedy Washington were with her. Olivia noticed that Elin's hair was even longer and wavier than before, only now it was topped with twisted-back braids and what looked to be a delicate crown, just like a princess.

Trying not to stare at Elin's hairstyle, Olivia glanced down at her legs instead. *Yuck!* Both girls had splotchy, reddish patches covered with calamine lotion. But as painful as that sight was, Olivia didn't give a hoot about the poison ivy mystery now. She had much bigger things to worry about. *What if these two find out about THREADS and Ethan asks them to join? Or worse, what if they just push their way in? We have to end this meeting right now.*

Elin wasted no time sizing up the room. "Hi, Austen," she said, slipping into the chair next to him, where Zoe had been sitting.

Right away, Kennedy reached into her pocket for her phone. "Hey, Elin and Austen, let me take a pic! Sooo stellar!" Elin fluffed up her hair and then leaned in close to Austen.

Then, Kennedy turned her attention to Ethan. "Hey, Ethan, let me take one with you," she squealed.

He jumped up. "I have to be going," he said, grabbing his backpack and skateboard.

Mu Mu nudged Olivia.

"We do too," Olivia said, her voice tight.

"Uh, bye," muttered Mu Mu over her shoulder as they bolted through the family room.

Ethan pushed open the front door. The porch was, like, ten degrees colder and soaked from the heavy rain. Before she could stop herself, Olivia stumbled over two open umbrellas blowing around the wet floor. She chased one and Mu Mu the other. On them in large, purple letters was written *MAGIC TRESSES*.

"Guess we know who these belong to, but yipes, this rain. We'll get soaked!" cried Mu Mu, snapping the umbrella shut. Olivia glanced over at Ethan.

He looks like he could care less about the rain, she thought.

"See you," he muttered, pulling the hood on his black-and-white Windbreaker low over his head and zooming off on his skateboard.

"Maybe we should wait here for a minute until it lets up?" suggested Mu Mu.

"Good idea," replied Olivia, leaning against the front door. "Only the sky looks really dark. We may be here for a while."

Mu tried to change the subject. "So, Elin and Kennedy… Didn't that look like poison ivy on their legs?" she said, wrinkling her nose.

"Maybe," muttered Olivia with a shrug, still bummed out by the idea of Elin worming her way into THREADS.

Mu Mu shrugged too. "Hey, is that your phone?" she asked.

Olivia looked down at a text. "OMG! I have to go. The roof at Katonah Crafts is leaking! Miss Ruth Ann needs help."

"Come on!" cried Mu Mu, racing into the rain.

The sign in the shop door window read *Closed* when the girls came panting in. Soggy boxes were piled every which way on the floor and tables. Much to their amazement, Ethan hurried in from the supply room with a large carton.

"Everything has to come out now," he shouted. "The roof inside is leaking!"

All three ran to the back. Olivia's heart sank when she saw Miss Ruth Ann trying to pack up everything. She looked overwhelmed, her face red and exhausted.

"We'll do that!" Olivia immediately cried out. "Mu Mu, can you take Miss Ruth Ann to the front?"

"No, no, I'll do this," protested Miss Ruth Ann. "But I still can't reach your mother."

"Please. Please, let us do it," said Olivia in a gentle voice while guiding her to the crafts table. "You keep trying Mom, OK?" she added and then dashed back to the supply room.

Ethan ran in for more cartons, and Olivia handed him one as drops of water fell on her head and shoulders.

It was gushing in from beneath the pressed metal panels of the old tin ceiling. Worried that the roof would give way, she started to work even faster.

A step stool was in the corner. She grabbed it and then reached up for the highest supplies, struggling with a carton marked *Bracelet Instructions* when a voice said, "I'll get that. You get the lower ones."

With a jerk, Olivia turned around to see Austen. She

jumped down and started carrying out boxes of beads and wires.

"Olivia, I keep trying and trying to reach your mother and your father," Miss Ruth Ann called to her in a worried voice.

Olivia realized how important it was to stay calm. This was a real emergency, and going to pieces would make it worse. "We know they went to White Plains for some supplies. Maybe there's bad reception on the Saw Mill Parkway?" she explained, stacking the boxes of beads and wires in a dry spot near the register. "They should be back soon. Don't worry. Everything will be OK."

The bell on the front door jingled, and Zoe hurried in. "I got Ethan's text. I had to wait for Press to get off his blog and watch Carl," she explained breathlessly. "What can I do?"

Olivia pointed toward the back of the shop.

"OK, let's make a line," Austen said when he saw his cousin had joined them. "I'll be on this end. Ethan, you be on the counter and tables?"

"Right," said Ethan, nodding.

"Olivia, you're next to me," Austen said while handing her a carton. "Then Mu Mu and Zoe."

It took only a short time before the last of the cartons and supplies were passed down the line.

"Good work," said Austen, jumping down from the step stool.

Olivia looked up at him. "Thank you. Thank you so much."

"Sure thing."

Before Olivia could reply, Ethan popped his head in. "Got everything?" he asked, looking around.

"Yup," Olivia and Austen said together.

"Sure?" Ethan persisted.

Austen shot him a look that said, "lighten up."

"Let me check on Miss Ruth Ann," Olivia said, sliding past them into the main part of the shop.

Miss Ruth Ann seemed more like her old self, busy showing everyone how to dry off the supplies and where to stack them. *What a relief!* They were almost done when thunder and lightning crackled through the skies. The overhead lights started flickering on and off.

"I'll get the flashlights," shouted Miss Ruth Ann, opening a drawer under the front counter.

"What about the generator?" Olivia called out.

The front door swung open. "Did you say generator? I've got it, Ollie," her father announced, holding the door for her mom.

"Miss Ruth Ann!" Olivia's mom called out when she saw all the cartons and the soggy mess her beloved manager had been forced to cope with.

Olivia's dad came prepared with a blue tarp and a big flashlight. "Come with me, young man," he said right away to Austen. "You can help with the generator. Then we'll get this tarp on the roof over the supply room."

"Yes, sir." Austen hurried behind him. In a few minutes, electricity from the generator came on. It wasn't full steam, but there was enough to power a light or two and the overhead fans, to help dry things out.

"Whew!" Olivia's dad shook off the rain from his jacket and stamped his feet when they came back in. "What a storm!" He closed the door to the supply room. "Everybody, please stay out of the back until the rain ends and we can inspect the roof. It will probably have to be replaced," he said, looking at Olivia's mom.

After making sure Miss Ruth Ann was all right, Olivia's mom had started to go over the supplies. "OK," she told Olivia's dad. "But I don't know how to thank you, everyone. And I don't know how you were able to do so much so fast."

"You can thank Miss Ruth Ann, Mom, and THREADS," said Olivia.

The members looked at each other, and like a flash, they realized the whole club was there.

"Guess we're a great team," said Zoe, holding out her arm with her THREADS bracelet. The other four members extended their arms with their bracelets too.

"One, two, three," said Zoe. Then all the members shouted, "THREADS! Yay!"

Olivia's mom, dad, and Miss Ruth Ann laughed.

"Two things," said Olivia's dad. "First, I want you to call or text your parents and let them know you're here. I'll drive you home when the rain lets up. And second, I'm going up the block for pizza. Nicolo's lights were on.

Mu Mu and Ollie, don't worry. I'll get yours cut up into small pieces, OK? So raise your hand if you're in."

Everyone's hands shot up.

"Need some help, Mr. Jones?" Austen asked as Olivia's dad opened the door.

He thought for a second and said, "Sure."

As Austen passed by Olivia on the way out, he whispered to her, "Ollie. Cool name."

"Thanks, Gus," she laughed back. She'd had that in her back pocket for a while now.

CHAPTER 27

Dams were bursting and water was gushing everywhere. It was getting higher and higher! Sullivan was barking!

With a start, Olivia awoke in the middle of the night. Sullivan was gently snoring in his bed on the floor. Everything was dry. Everything was OK. *Whew!*

Olivia plumped up her pillow, tried to find a cool spot in the sheets for her feet, and then closed her eyes.

He knows my nickname, she thought. *But wait! I didn't even think about my braces. Austen saw them. He had to have noticed! And he was still nice to me. Great, this so cool. I will tough this out! But what about THREADS? We are a good team... But wait! How did Austen know to come to the shop? Did Ethan text him too? And what happened with Elin and Kennedy and the poison ivy? So many mysteries...*

The next morning was bright and beautiful. *God's in His heaven. All's right with the world*, Olivia thought at first, but then she remembered the damage to Katonah Crafts and hurried downstairs to see if she could help her mother.

As Olivia walked into the family room, her phone buzzed with a group text from Austen. Mom wants 2 meet w THREADS Mon or Tues?

Things were happening! Last night, when her dad gave everyone a ride home, Olivia and Zoe had tagged along. Ethan had insisted on going on his skateboard, so he left right after pizza.

When her dad drove into North Salem, it was still dark from the storm, so Olivia couldn't get a really good look at where Mu Mu and Austen lived except that both had houses that were set way back from the road. In front of Austen's was a horse corral and a sign hanging from a tree that said *Horizon Farm*. When they pulled up the hill to the house, she could see it was old, like George Washington old, a long, low farmhouse with lots of additions and probably a great view.

Mu Mu's place by contrast was huge and new, with soaring peaks and lots of glass and stone and a garage so big it looked like a car dealership.

But both properties were pretty far away from their neighbors. And there were no sidewalks, not at all like Katonah village, where all the houses were nestled right next each other. *Still, it's going to be cool to visit*, she thought. *I wonder if Austen has his own horse.*

There was too much work to do at Katonah Crafts, so Olivia decided to put off her Skype with Alex. Big storm last night. TTYL , she texted instead.

When Olivia and her mom arrived at the shop, Miss Ruth Ann was already sorting through the feathers, buttons, bells, and charms. Windows were open, fans were on, and a roofer was on his way.

Olivia's mom taped off the back of the shop, where her dad had piled the cartons earlier in the morning, and, at ten o'clock, asked Olivia to flip over the *Closed* sign on the front door to *Open*.

When she pulled back the curtain, she looked down on Ethan sitting on the front stoop. *What's he doing here?*

She hurried back to her mother and Miss Ruth Ann. "Ethan is outside," she whispered.

"Yes, I know," said Miss Ruth Ann. "He gets here early on Saturdays."

"Really? On Saturdays?" Olivia marveled.

"Come in, Ethan," her mom called out with a bright smile. "Oh, Olivia, sweetie, we need more of those big, black garbage bags and paper towels. Can you run down to Village Hardware and get some?"

"Sure, Mom," said Olivia, picking up her bag.

"That's going to be heavy. Are you sure you can carry all that back?" asked Miss Ruth Ann. "Ethan, can you be an angel and go with Olivia?"

Ethan looked like a trapped animal, but he went along.

The two headed down Main Street, toward the hardware store two blocks away. A minute passed in silence. A long minute.

"So, Ethan, are you going away this summer?" Olivia finally asked, desperate for something to say.

"Away? Like where? You mean like Paris or something?" he said sort of sarcastically.

"No, I meant like on a vacation or to sleepaway camp," Olivia muttered, her voice trailing off.

"Nope," he said, shaking his head.

Village Hardware was busy when they walked in. *Guess there was a lot of storm cleanup*, Olivia figured.

"I'll wait outside by the door," Ethan said, pulling his baseball cap low. Olivia noticed it had a NASA insignia. *That's kind of cool*, she thought.

After she'd gotten everything up on the front counter, Olivia asked the shop's owner, Mr. Dalwinkle, to charge it to her mother's account.

A pleasant-faced, gray-haired man with a manner as sweet as the jar of candies next to the register, he looked down at her and smiled. "Will do," he said, taking a pencil out of the pocket of his long apron that said *Village Hardware* and making a note on a pad. "And you have a good day," he added. "Jayden, come up here and carry these things down to Katonah Crafts for this young lady."

A muscular boy about fourteen years old came forward and picked up the bulging shopping bags. He was tall, with thick black hair and pale-blue eyes. Olivia couldn't remember ever seeing him before.

"Oh, that's OK, Mr. Dalwinkle," said Olivia, pointing toward the front where Ethan was stationed outside. "I have help."

"Then take these to the front, Jayden," said the owner, who added, "and, Olivia, please give my very best to Miss Ruth Ann."

"Sure will. Thanks!" replied Olivia, walking away with Jayden following behind.

Ethan seemed to be very absorbed watching the traffic when the two came out.

"Hey, nerd bro, is that you?" Jayden immediately shouted.

"Yeah, hi," said Ethan in a low voice.

"Wait! Is this *the* Olivia?" cried Jayden, spinning to look at her.

"Could you keep your voice down?" growled Ethan. Olivia had never seen him look so uncomfortable.

"Yup, that's me. Olivia," she answered.

"Whoa, bro. Good work," said Jayden with a smirk.

"So, Olivia, you're the one whose mom owns the crafts shop down the street? Maybe I'll drop by there later, make sure Thread Head here is behaving himself."

Ethan grabbed the bags from Jayden's hands. "Let's go," he said to Olivia and then hurried down the street.

"Wait up, Ethan," she cried. "Who was that?" she asked, catching up to him.

"Nobody," replied Ethan.

"Nobody? Come on, who was that?"

"Will you stop? Just my stupid stepbrother, if you have to know," Ethan said and walked inside Katonah Crafts.

"Oh," said Olivia thinking, *Guess they're not BFFs.*

Miss Ruth Ann was waiting for the paper towels. "I need to spread out some of the supplies, like the cords, leathers, suede, hemp, and all those pearls," she told Olivia. "And then I can make a proper count of what we lost. There is insurance."

"I'll help you," Olivia volunteered. "Oh, and by the way, Mr. Dalwinkle, you know, from Village Hardware? He especially said to say hello to you."

Miss Ruth Ann looked surprised and then a little

embarrassed. "Well, thank you, Olivia," she murmured and then turned her attention back to her work.

Olivia went into the supply room where Ethan was standing on a stool, restacking some fresh, dry cartons. "Hey, stupid, why did you have to tell Miss Ruth Ann that?" he said, pitching a fit right away.

"What! What are you talking about?"

"Duh, does everything have to be spelled out for you?" he asked. "Let Mr. Dalwinkle deliver his own stupid messages. You put Miss Ruth Ann on the spot."

"I did not! What's wrong with you?" Olivia shot back, her face turning red.

"Here's a good idea: Why don't you think before you say anything?" he snarled.

"Stop it! You're such a control freak, and you're just losing it because of your stupid stepbrother."

"Shut up! You don't know what you're talking about!" cried Ethan, jumping down from the stool and getting in her face.

Olivia's mom came rushing in. "Please, you two! Keep your voices down. There are customers in front. Oh, and,

Ethan, thank you again for being such a big help. Why, I should give you a job," she said.

"Great! And then maybe Thread Head could live here too!" cried Olivia, running from the shop in tears.

CHAPTER 28

It wasn't until the next morning that Olivia pulled up a chair in front of the computer for her Skype date. She'd had a terrible night and had only just apologized to her mom before coming down.

"It was just growing pains, Ollie, sweetie, that's all," said her mom, giving her daughter a kiss on the cheek.

Still, she felt bad about calling Ethan "Thread Head." She tried to tell herself he had it coming, but that didn't make it better.

A minute later, Alex's face filled the screen.

"Guess what! Guess what!" she cried. "Fabien asked if he could walk me home. Of course, I have to check with Maman first, but maybe she'll let me. I hope so. The school is only a few blocks away, and there are no busy streets to cross."

"Super!" Olivia cried.

"So when is your meeting at the hospital?" Alex asked.

"Tomorrow after camp. Mom is driving us. But she's not coming in. She says THREADS is our thing."

"Well, that's cool. I'm sure you're completely prepared. You have lots of samples and your outline was really good."

"We're prepared," Olivia said. "But, Alex, I had this big fight with Ethan."

"With Ethan? What about?"

Before Olivia could answer, the screen started flashing and the image died.

Bummer, thought Olivia. *I wanted to ask her which bracelets she thought I should wear.*

CHAPTER 29

Olivia kept twisting the friendship bracelets on her arm, the blue-and-white one from her mom's friend Dawn and the one from THREADS. She couldn't remember ever being this nervous. Maybe it was from that awful fight with Ethan. And she hadn't spoken with him since. But, on the plus side, at least she wouldn't have to say much, if anything, at the meeting. After all, THREADS was Ethan's idea. He would want to speak for them.

Austen's mother was running late, and the five of them had been sitting in a hallway at the Central Hospital for fifteen minutes. Mu Mu had brought along a paperback book, *The Universe's Fifty Most Insane Chocolate-Chip Cookie Recipes*, and was completely absorbed in it.

"I'm trying to find the greatest chocolate-chip cookie recipe ever," she explained.

"A noble quest," joked Austen.

Olivia looked over at him and smiled. She liked his turn of phrase, "a noble quest."

"So, what's Carl up to?" Austen asked Zoe.

"Oh, let me show these new pics from breakfast this morning," she said, reaching for her phone. "Press is teaching him to sit for biscuits."

Everyone was cool except for Ethan. He was starting to lose it. He got up and paced back and forth. Finally he blurted out, "Hey, Austen, maybe you should ask if your mom is actually going to see us today?"

"Cool it, Ethan. She'll be ready soon. You can't get thrown off your game because of a short wait." His phone buzzed. He looked down and clicked it off. "Maybe we should all turn off our phones?" he suggested.

The inner door opened and out walked a tall, slender woman with light-blond hair just like Austen's.

"Hello, everybody," she said. "Please come in. I am so sorry for the delay, but I wanted Ginny Johnson to sit in on the meeting with us. She's our patient advocate and her input will be very valuable."

Olivia thought, *Wow! This sounds pretty official. Hope Ethan can handle it.*

Austen introduced everyone, and then they walked down a wide hallway to a conference room with a long table.

"Let's all sit down at this end," said Mrs. Dodd. "Oh, and here comes Ginny Johnson now. Ginny, this is the group of young people I was telling you about. They call themselves THREADS, and they have an idea that might be very effective for our patients."

Ginny gave each of them a warm smile and sat down. "Well, thank you for coming. Who would like to start?"

No one answered.

Ginny Johnson looked down at her notes and said, "Mrs. Dodd has informed me that THREADS was the brainchild of Ethan Fleckman. I assume that's you, young man?" she said looking at Ethan. "Would you like to walk us through how THREADS would work for our patients here at Central Hospital?"

"Uh, Mrs. Johnson, Olivia Jones is in charge of that—of our communications. She made up the charts and flyers," Ethan replied, pointing in Olivia's direction.

Olivia's blood ran cold. *I have to speak? I'm not even prepared!* This was, like, the *worst* moment of her life! Beyond the worst! In a galaxy far, far, away the worst! Why didn't she realize this would happen?

"Well," she said, but her voice was high pitched and squeaky. "Well," she started over, "here are the flyers which explain what THREADS is and how it works. And here are some samples of our finished bracelets." She stood up and walked over to where Austen's mother was sitting with Mrs. Johnson and laid the bracelets out in three groups.

"These are our easy samples, these medium, and these advanced," she said, pointing to each group. "Our idea is to visit patients and bring along our supplies and some samples. They can choose if they want to make bracelets and we can help them, or they can take one that's already made. My mother, I mean Katonah Crafts, is donating all the materials."

Mrs. Johnson picked up every bracelet. "This idea is

very clever," she finally said to Mrs. Dodd. "It offers a range of involvement."

"And there's another aspect of this too," pointed out Mrs. Dodd. "I remember from my own childhood that friendship bracelets can also have messages, right? I especially like that you thought to make a chart about the meanings of the various colors. It expresses hope and establishes a connection. Well done."

"Thank you," said Olivia, waving her hand at the other members. "We're really a team, and we can work our visiting times around your schedule."

All the members of THREADS nodded in agreement.

"Let's start next Monday. I'll line up volunteers to be with each of you during the initial patient visit. Are you available in the afternoon, say at two o'clock?" asked Ginny Johnson.

"Yes!" they all shouted.

Five minutes later, they were walking out the doors and into the public parking lot.

"It worked, Mom!" cried Olivia. "We're official. We make our first visit next Monday!"

"Come on, everybody," said Zoe, putting her hand out as if to create a huddle. "Let's go!"

Just like after the flood, they all put their hands together and cried, "THREADS! Yay!"

"Well, this deserves some ice cream," announced Olivia's mom, opening the car door. "All aboard for Katonah Cones!"

CHAPTER 30

Cookies, cookies. Milk-chocolate-chip cookies, butterscotch, or dark chocolate? Milk chocolate chip, butterscotch, or dark chocolate?

It was a hard choice for Mu Mu.

She remembered what her Grandma Cam always told her, "Never serve a new dish to company without trying it out first." But she'd promised Zoe she would bring something to the next meeting of THREADS, which was in a little more than two hours.

This is no time to be timid, she thought. *I'll make a cookie combo. Yeah! Put all three kinds of chips in them and just go for it!*

The sprawling kitchen next to the enormous family room, with its soaring, double-height ceiling, was quiet.

Her mom was working at her office in town, and her dad was on his way to Los Angeles on another business trip. Best of all, Chris, her dopey brother, had shipped off to sleepaway camp for a whole month. Heaven!

The oven door echoed in the space that was so big Chris always talked about hanging a basketball hoop off the balcony. Actually, Mu Mu always thought that was a cool idea, because with its light-wood floors, the family room did resemble a gym. Her dad put up the hoop in the backyard instead, right in front of the skateboard ramp he had built.

When the cookies come out of the oven, they had a chunky, chewy, gooey look that checked a few boxes for Mu Mu on her noble quest. She was a patient cook, and when the cookies had completely cooled, she slipped them into a container and then climbed up the winding staircase to the wide balcony that ran outside the bedrooms.

Rays of sunlight were making her room positively glow. Every time she saw the bright-pink walls, she had to smile and knew she made the right choice. But, for the first time, it occurred to her: *What would Olivia's color chart say this means, "sweet and soft"? Like cotton candy, maybe?*

Time was short. There were only a few minutes to inspect her braces and get her long, straight hair up into braids. Austen said he would swing by on his way to Zoe's house in the village and pick her up, so that was good. Her mom still didn't know about Carl, and so far Mu Mu hadn't had a problem keeping it that way. Her mom wasn't big on secrets, but this one was different.

She opened her desk drawer and reached for a small, braided jewelry bowl in the back. Inside was the pink-and-green neckband she had made with the name *CARL*. Mu Mu held the band gently, remembering how she had tried it on the little pup the week before he was supposed to come home with them. *We loved the name Carl too. Funny that Zoe kept that.*

Her backpack was hanging on the doorknob. It was too hard to throw away the band but also too hard to keep it. Reaching for the bag, she told herself, *I know, I'll take it to Zoe's. It will only fit Carl for a little while anyway.*

Slinging the backpack over her shoulder, she headed

downstairs for the cookies and then out to the front, where the lawn guys were blowing the clippings and leaves from the long, winding driveway.

"Hey, Mike. Hey, Joe. How are you?" she shouted with a wave and hurried over to them with a small bag of her cookies.

Their faces lit up.

"Wow! Chocolate chip, thanks, Mu Mu. Hey, there's your ride," said Mike as Austen's brother Ryan stopped his pickup truck at the curb.

"Hi, Ryan. Hi, Austen," she said, opening the back door and hopping in. "Thanks for the lift. Who would like a triple-chip cookie?"

Austen and his brother laughed. "Sounds great," said Austen. "Was this recipe in your book?"

"Sort of," said Mu Mu, chewing away. "Hey, you know these *are* good."

"Yeah, they are," agreed Austen. "Hope you brought a lot." Before Mu Mu could answer, his phone buzzed with a text. He looked down and then clicked it off.

"Hey, Gus, who's Elin? Another one of your

girlfriends?" Ryan started to tease him. "Mu Mu, what do girls see in this guy?"

Mu Mu laughed but quickly turned her attention to what was outside the window. Her body tensed up. She knew it was just around the bend, right past the reservoir. *Oh no, there it is.* "Golden's Bridge Goldens."

With a silent sigh, she thought, *Wonder how long it will be before I pass that sign and not be totally bummed out.*

CHAPTER 31

Olivia had no choice but to get over the Ethan episode. Seriously. She only hoped he was wrong about her embarrassing Miss Ruth Ann. That was something she would never ever want to do.

Her dressing room at Get Ups was piled high with shorts and tops. A little while ago, Olivia's mom gave her one of her credit cards and said in a very serious voice, "Ask them to call me if there are any problems. But I know Marcie, so everything should be OK. Try the things on in the shop, but then try them on again at home, and don't cut off the tags until you're absolutely sure."

As Olivia pulled on a pink-and-blue polka-dot top with a lace insert, she made a promise to do something nice for Miss Ruth Ann. Maybe stop at Katonah

Cupcakes on her way back? Or at Stems and Vines, her favorite flower shop? She had seen some very sweet, tiny roses displayed outside there that morning, and she had the last of her birthday money tucked in her backpack.

Suddenly, she heard a lot of giggling and the sound of approaching footsteps.

Someone yanked back the curtain.

Olivia gasped.

"Oh, sorry!" said the salesperson, her arm loaded with clothes. "This way, miss," she said, turning to her customer, who was Elin Pierson, with her faithful buddy Kennedy Washington. Today Elin was wearing a big boho headband with actual feathers dangling from it. Olivia thought, *Maybe she's a Native American? Probably not.*

Elin rolled her eyes at Kennedy, and they marched into the dressing room next door.

Distracted, Olivia closed the curtain and reached for a short, yellow skirt with a print of butterflies edged with a pink ruffle. Olivia's mom had seen it in the shop window and thought it would look good on her.

But then Olivia froze. She couldn't concentrate. All she could think of was Elin making fun of her. At the very moment she decided to bail, a phone rang.

"Oh, hi, Austen," Elin nearly shouted. "Sorry I didn't answer your texts. I'm busy now. Can you call me back later? How about at four? I should be free then. OK, bye."

Olivia heard more giggling, picked up the clothes, and rushed to the front counter. *That's it. I'm out of here*, she said to herself. She was about to buy nothing at all when a text from Zoe came through: Tennis @ 3?

OK, Olivia texted back.

She looked at the pile of clothes and raised her chin. *I'm not going to get run out of here*, she thought. *Especially by someone wearing a feathered headdress, like Elin.*

"I'll take this pink top, this blue one, and the white, and these white shorts and the skirt with the ruffle too," she told the young woman at the register and then fished out her mother's credit card.

"Come again," called out the assistant as Olivia left the shop.

Halfway down the block, in front of Stems and Vines, she stopped. There were two bouquets of the tiny, red roses left on the display stand. She picked them up and headed inside. She had enough money to buy one for Miss Ruth Ann and one for her mom. Then she dashed back up the street to Katonah Crafts. She didn't want to be late for her tennis with Zoe.

★ • ★ • ★

The courts were busy when they rode up. "Do you mind waiting?" her friend asked.

"Nope," said Olivia, sitting down at a nearby picnic table. "Wish I had some more of those triple-chip cookies Mu Mu made yesterday."

"Yeah! Who knew she was so good at baking?" said Zoe. "Hey, but we got a lot done besides eating cookies. That was a smart idea of yours to photograph all the bracelets. Guess we didn't think about how we were actually going to show the samples to the patients."

"Well, I realized that we would need five identical sets, and who has time to make all those?"

"Maybe Ethan?" joked Zoe. "Oh, look, they've

finished," she said, pointing to two young boys walking off a court. "Let's go!"

After a couple of quick games, the girls decided to take a break and headed for some boulders under the shade of a tall oak tree.

Zoe took a big sip of water from her bottle. "So, Olivia, is Ethan always so moody?" she asked.

"Yup," laughed Olivia. "Seems like he's getting moodier."

"Oh, look. There he is."

"Ethan?" said Olivia, swiveling around.

"No, Austen. He said he would try to meet us here before four o'clock," said Zoe, standing up and waving.

"Four?" murmured Olivia, remembering Elin's loud conversation in Get Ups, the one she couldn't help overhearing.

"Yeah, well, it's a little before," said Zoe, looking at her phone.

Olivia couldn't believe it. Was Austen actually going to call Elin in front of them? *Well, let him*, she thought. *I'm not leaving!*

Austen pedaled over and propped his bike up against the tree. Then he brushed off his tank top and cargo pants. Olivia noticed he was still wearing the Mega Diamond XXOO friendship bracelet around his ankle.

"Did you bike all the way into town from your house?" asked Zoe.

"I wish," said Austen. "Ryan bashed my bike up last week showing off for his girlfriend, and I just got it back from Lou's Bike Repair, you know, on the way out of town? Ryan's picking me up later. Can I meet him at your house?"

"Sure, that's cool," said Zoe, standing up. "But I have to go. Remember, Press and I are taking Carl to the vet for his checkup at four thirty. I can't be late."

"OK," asked Austen. "Hey, Olivia, want to play me?" He pointed to the courts.

"Sure," she said, getting to her feet.

"Can I borrow your racket, Zoe? I'll drop it off after." Zoe tossed it to him and rode off.

"OK, Ollie, let's see what you've got," said Austen, trotting to the court.

"Try to keep up with me, Gus," Olivia laughed.

The next hour flew by, and finally, totally wiped out, they collapsed on the side of the court.

They both stretched out their legs and sat in silence for a few moments. "Look, your legs are almost as long as mine," said Austen, pointing.

"Well, maybe in addition to beating you at tennis, I'll be taller than you too," Olivia laughed.

"Really? You think so?" said Austen, grinning. "Sorry I'm so grungy," he added, looking down at his cargo shorts. "I've been working at the community garden."

"Wow," said Olivia. *That's a pretty cool thing to do*, she thought.

"Maybe you would like to come see it? It's just off Pawley Road, you know, by the old train stop?"

Olivia was thrilled. Maybe her mom could drive her sometime? Sometime soon?

Before she could answer, Austen's phone rang.

"OK, Ryan, I'll be right there," he said, standing up. He reached down and gave her his hand, saying, "My brother is at Zoe's. I've got to go."

"I'll go too." Olivia picked up her bike and followed him down the trail leading out of the park. She had to smile. Four o'clock had come and gone with no Elin phone call.

When they reached her house, she hopped off her bike and waved good-bye. Austen waved back. She noticed the big smile he gave her. What she didn't notice was Elin and Kennedy standing at the corner of Bedford Road, staring at them. And they were definitely *not* smiling.

CHAPTER 32

"OK, Team Unicorn, I want you to bring up the rear, right behind Team Dolphin. And, teams, stay together. But let's keep an eye out for pinecones so we can make wreaths later. Everybody got their bags?"

Ashley, the counselor, and Parker, the CIT, were organizing the eleven/twelve girls for a nature walk. Mr. Kapoor, the sixth grade science teacher from Alexander Hamilton Middle School, had volunteered to take them on a trek through Carey's Woods, a large woodland preserve that abutted Monroe Park.

Most of the girls were excited and set off chattering happily, but Olivia noticed that Elin and Kennedy seemed extra-bored and were lagging behind them.

That's too bad, she thought, *because it's an incredible*

day. When she looked up and saw the golden-yellow sunlight bursting through the leaves and the limbs of the trees, she couldn't help thinking of a favorite poem of her father's: "I think that I shall never see, A poem as lovely as a tree." Gazing at the upward-reaching branches, she realized exactly what the poet Joyce Kilmer meant by a tree that "lifts her leafy arms to pray."

The deep shade of the forest refreshed the campers as they tramped on. A well-worn path led them past trees that were marked with plaques where Mr. Kapoor stopped and filled them in on the various characteristics.

Olivia had never been this far into the woods, and she noticed there was a lot of debris on the sides of the path, especially some immense trees that had fallen with their huge root balls exposed. From the back of the group, she asked Mr. Kapoor why they were there.

"Great question," said the teacher. "Anyone here know the answer? Anyone? Anyone?"

Nobody spoke up until Mu Mu shouted out, "Leftovers from Hurricane Sandy?"

"Yes, that's right!" he replied with a smile. "And

because this is a woodland, and not a park in a residential area, most of these fallen trees will stay here and eventually decay."

Olivia gave Mu Mu a fist bump, and the group made its way to the next spot.

They came to a large open area with a huge, thick carpet of green leaves covering the woodland floor on one side of the path. "Now, campers, I would like you all to stand well back from this," Mr. Kapoor warned them while waving his arm. "Observe carefully *Toxicodendron radicans*, or what is its common name?"

"Poison ivy," Mu Mu and Olivia said together.

"That's right, poison ivy. It can grow along the ground or on trees. Pay particular attention now. If you look over there at those thick vines twining up the oak tree… Yes, the nasty-looking ones with the reddish hairs. They can all cause a severe poison ivy outbreak."

Mu Mu nudged Olivia and rolled her eyes toward Elin and Kennedy.

"Campers, remember what your counselor told you?" asked Mr. Kapoor.

"Leaves of three, let it be," they all shouted.

At that precise moment, Olivia and Mu Mu cried, "*Ooh!*" Before they could stop themselves, they fell forward right into the dense bed of poison ivy.

All of their exposed skin, their hands, faces, arms, and legs, had made direct contact with the plants.

"Girls! Girls! Get out of there at once!" shouted the teacher.

Olivia and Mu Mu struggled to their feet as Mr. Kapoor snapped out, "Everyone, back to the camp right away! Stay on the path. You two walk in front of me. Quickly."

Olivia looked over at Mu Mu. Her face was drained of color. "Are you OK? Did you get hurt?" she asked.

Mu Mu shook her head and walked even faster.

"Do you two live nearby?" Mr. Kapoor asked as they hurried along the path. "You must shower immediately. Use plenty of soap to try to get every last bit of the urushiol oil off. That's what causes the rash. Wash your hair, your clothes, and your shoes. Don't touch any surface directly before showering. Use a paper towel if necessary. And stay away from pets. You could wipe the oil onto their fur."

"Call my mother," Olivia shouted to Parker when they hit the camp. "Tell her what happened."

"You have to come home with me," said Olivia to Mu Mu. Together, they raced toward the bike rack. "Hop on the back. We have no choice."

Mu Mu put her arms around Olivia's waist and the two sped off. When they turned onto Edgemont Road, they saw Olivia's mom standing on the front porch. She'd already been on the Internet and was prepared for them.

"Sullivan is out back," she said. "Just throw down your bike. The showers are on. Olivia, you go in mine. Mu Mu, you use the hall bath. There are bags on the floor for your clothes and, Mu Mu, I have put out some of Olivia's things for you to wear. Don't worry. You can probably wash off all the oil."

CHAPTER 33

In twelve to forty-eight hours, a reaction usually develops.

That was what the pharmacist told Olivia's mom later that afternoon when she was stocking up on lotion, gauze pads, oatmeal bath products, and anything else that might help.

Mu Mu's mom was taking more of a wait-and-see attitude. After she picked up Mu Mu from Olivia's, they swung by the supermarket. Her mom ran in and got lots of ingredients for more chocolate-chip cookies. Mrs. Lin was realistic. She worried Mu Mu would go batty if she was confined to the house and couldn't cook.

Meanwhile, both girls stayed in contact.

"This is already such a pain!" moaned Mu Mu over

the phone later that night. "My Grandma Cam keeps making me drink chicken broth!"

Olivia laughed. "My mom wants to know if you have enough craft supplies to keep busy. She'll bring you whatever you want."

Mu Mu looked at her desk, where skeins of flosses were already laid out. "Thanks. That's nice of her, but I'm cool. I think I'll make a Dream Catcher bracelet. I saw one on a girl in Dr. Justin's office and found the instructions online. If it works out, I'll make one for you."

"Sounds super," said Olivia, wondering what she could do for Mu Mu in return.

"But you know, Olivia, I can't help thinking that Elin and Kennedy pushed us," Mu Mu added. "They were right behind us."

"OMG! No! Even Elin wouldn't go that far!" cried Olivia, unwilling to admit out loud what she was already thinking.

Mu Mu paused and then said, "Come on. How else did we both wind up in the poison ivy at the same time? Mom has a call in to Ashley. I'll let you know how that goes."

"OK."

Olivia hung up and looked around her room. She didn't feel any different, no fever or anything like that, but she was really worried. She didn't want to be a total downer and tell Mu Mu that if they did break out in a rash, there went their visit to Central Hospital with THREADS. *But Mu Mu is sharp. She's probably figured that out already*, she thought. *And we'll know soon. Probably by tomorrow morning.*

"Knock, knock," said her mom in a cheerful voice, coming in with Olivia's laundered clothes and shoes. "I've washed these three times, sweetie. They should be perfectly fine," she said, putting them on a chair in the corner. Still, Olivia couldn't help looking at them with dread.

"And here is your friendship bracelet," she said, handing her the wide band that said *THREADS*. "Maybe you shouldn't put it on until tomorrow in case there is a rash?"

"OK, Mom. But wait! Where is the blue-and-white bracelet? The one you gave me? The one from Dawn?" she asked with alarm.

Her mom blinked and seemed puzzled. "I didn't see it, sweetie. But I'll check the washing machine."

Olivia followed her into the laundry room off the kitchen. The washer and dryer were empty. They even checked the lint filter.

"Could it have slipped off?" Olivia's mom wondered. "When you fell? And how *did* you and Mu Mu both fall at the same moment?"

Olivia sank down onto a bench. This was too much to handle. First, the poison ivy, and now the missing bracelet. She needed the bracelet back! Everything had been better since her mom gave it to her: THREADS, Austen, Zoe, Mu Mu, the puppy, even Ethan! Would it all just go downhill now?

"Mom, I have to have it!" she cried, looking frantic.

"Oh, Ollie, calm down. We'll find it. First, you ask Mu Mu if maybe it's mixed in with her things," her mother said hopefully.

Olivia raced back upstairs for her phone.

Mu Mu picked up on the first ring. "Nope. My clothes are right here. I'll check them again. Nope, nothing. But

I did find out something else. I wasn't sure if I should tell you."

"What?" asked Olivia, half listening.

"Ashley told my mom that one of the other campers, Tiffany Diaz, you know, from Team Chestnut, recorded our fall. She was taking pics of the poison ivy and caught the whole thing."

Olivia had a bad feeling about what was coming next.

"It was Elin and Kennedy. They pushed us. Check your phone. Tiffany is sending the video now."

Olivia hung up and immediately opened Tiffany's message. The video showed them being pushed, plain as day.

Tears filled her eyes. There had been mean-girl stuff before, but this was the worst! She was crazy to think things had gotten better.

She ran downstairs and out the side door.

Olivia's mom followed, grabbed her by the shoulders, and looked into her daughter's stricken face. "What is it, sweetie?" her mom wanted to know.

Olivia couldn't bear to tell her the truth, that someone would do something so awful to her.

Instead, she said with a sob, "I have to find the friendship bracelet. Will you help me?"

"Of course," her mom said. "Get in the car. We'll retrace your steps. Don't worry. Things just don't disappear!"

CHAPTER 34

"No, Dad. Don't do that. It's gone. We already looked all over the roads."

"Ollie, Mom has told me how important the bracelet is to you," her dad said, pulling on his tall rubber boots. He stood up and reached for his car keys. "If the bracelet is up in Carey's Woods, I'll find it. There's still plenty of daylight. I know you and Mom looked for a long time, but I'll put a pair of fresh eyes on it."

Olivia so wished he wouldn't. Her dad was allergic to poison ivy and could blow up like a balloon if he was exposed to it.

She turned to her mother. "Mom, make Dad stop. I'll be OK. Honest. I'll…I'll make another one."

"Daddy knows what he's doing, sweetie," her mom

said. "Let me bring in Sully, so he can go upstairs with you, Ollie."

Oh no, thought Olivia. *Things have gotten totally crazy! It's all my fault.*

Her mom opened the back door and clapped her hands. Sullivan pranced in, trying to scoot upstairs before anyone noticed that he had something in his mouth. A blue-and-white something.

"Look!" screamed Olivia. "Sully has the bracelet!"

"Drop it," commanded her dad in a firm voice.

Sullivan looked up as if to say, *Who, me?* but then he let it fall to the floor.

"Good boy!" said Olivia's dad.

Grabbing a paper towel, her mom scooped up the bracelet and put it in the bathroom sink to be washed later.

"Come on, Sully," she told the dog, opening the back door again. "Now, it's your turn for a bath. So far, so good, but we can't take any chances with poison ivy."

★ • ★ • ★

The rash started out small, and by the next evening,

Olivia had never been so bummed. She couldn't stop looking at her arms and legs, where each hour seemed to bring a new area of misery.

Her face was the worst, with nasty, red splotches threatening to become nastier and bigger.

For Mu Mu, her hands were driving her the most crazy. The soft spaces in between her slender fingers had become raw and sore.

"This totally sucks!" she cried. "You know it means we can't go with THREADS on Monday?"

Olivia was way ahead of that breaking news. Earlier, she'd texted Zoe, Ethan, and Austen.

"And Mom says I can't bake! This is so gross!" Mu Mu added for good measure.

Olivia wished there was something she could say to cheer up her friend, but she knew how useless that would sound. "Send me pics," she said instead, knowing she was the only person right then who could really understand the mess they were in.

Her mom knocked on her door.

"Ethan is here," she whispered.

"Make him go away, Mom. Please. I can't handle it!"

Her mom shrugged and went downstairs.

"Who's there?" asked Mu Mu.

"Only Ethan," Olivia said. "I don't know why he's here."

"Maybe he's trying to be nice? Talk to you later."

CHAPTER 35

A few yucky and itchy days went by.

Olivia Skyped with Alex, who was totally shocked by what had happened.

And she and Mu Mu shared their misery in endless texts. When she wasn't organizing and reorganizing her room, she was propped up on the sofa in the family room, where she and Sully got to binge watch whole seasons of TV shows. *That is the only good part*, she thought.

Every day, Austen and Zoe texted and asked to visit, but Olivia was certainly not up for that.

Late Monday afternoon, their friends sent Olivia and Mu Mu lots of pics of the first THREADS visit to the hospital. Olivia had to smile. Everybody wanted to take a selfie with Austen, both the nurses and the patients. There was even one of him with a man who had a mop and bucket. *And why not?* she thought. *He looks so cute in his blue-and-white shirt.*

By Tuesday afternoon, both she and Mu Mu could report no new breakouts, so the end of their ordeal was in sight, except for the Elin and Kennedy thing. Olivia dreaded ever facing them again.

"Yuck! Did you get their get-well card yet?" asked Mu Mu when she called before dinner.

"It just came a little while ago," Olivia replied. "The one with a Band-Aid on the front?"

"Yeah, and does it say 'OUCH' in big, red letters?"

"Yup," said Olivia. "Guess they sent us the same card."

Mu Mu dropped her voice. "Dad's back from his business trip, and he wants Camp Monroe to kick them out. He's furious."

"Really?" Olivia replied, feeling alarmed.

"Yeah, really. But, Olivia, Dad wants to talk to your parents first," Mu Mu explained. "Later tonight."

Olivia gulped. "I still haven't told them what happened.

They probably think I tripped and took you down with me. I'm kind of a klutz."

"No, you're not! But listen, maybe you better tell them," suggested Mu Mu, "so they don't hear it from Dad first?"

Yipes! This felt worse than ever. She was the one who got hurt, and now she had to go through the whole episode all over again?

At dinner, she started to tell her mom and dad about Mu Mu's call.

"Her father wants to speak with you," Olivia said, cutting her cheese ravioli into small pieces.

"I hope Mu Mu is getting better," said her mom. "But why does Mr. Lin want to speak with us?"

"Because, well, I didn't tell you…" Olivia trailed off.

"Sweetie, tell us what?" said her mom.

She looked down and said in a quiet voice, "That Mu Mu and I didn't fall. We were pushed. By Elin Pierson and Kennedy Washington."

"What?" cried her mom.

Olivia's dad put down his fork and wiped his mouth with his napkin.

"It gets worse," said Olivia, her red face turning even redder. "There's a video of it." Still she couldn't look up, and the rest of the story gushed out. "I just didn't want it to go viral and then everybody would know me as the dopey girl who got thrown into a bed of poison ivy. Then I would be the person someone hates so much they would do something horrible like that to me!"

Her dad pushed his plate away. Olivia raised her eyes. She could tell he was really angry. The vein in his forehead looked as if it were about to explode.

"Don't worry, Ollie," he said in a calm, controlled voice. "I know you and Mu Mu have been suffering, but now this is also about those other girls and what they did. They must be held accountable for their actions. Otherwise, they'll think it's OK to do unacceptable things like this. You understand?"

Olivia nodded.

"OK," said her dad. "Now tell us everything."

"*They're kicked out,*" reported Mu Mu. "Ashley just called my dad and said Heather, the camp director, decided. So...you don't have to tell your parents."

Olivia looked up at the ceiling and almost laughed.

"Too late! Dad got off the phone with Heather a little while ago. I heard him. Now he's calling Elin's and Kennedy's parents. He wants them to come to his office, and he's hoping your parents will come too."

"Wow! But that's a good thing, right? And at least we won't have to see the rest of Team Unicorn when we go back."

"Yeah, probably," replied Olivia. But she couldn't stop thinking, *Why do I still feel so bad? I have to stop being such a wuss.*

She glanced down at her left arm. Her wrist was healing fast. Soon, she could wear her friendship bracelets... and maybe they could go to camp the day after tomorrow or at least by Friday.

CHAPTER 36

Ethan studied the get-well-soon diamond-braided bracelet. He hoped it was girlie enough.

Yesterday, Miss Ruth Ann had helped him pick out the colors, all happy ones—fluorescent green, yellow, turquoise, and pink—and suggested he use tiny pink beads, one-eighth of an inch size, to make a border down the sides.

Maybe Olivia won't even want it. Maybe it will remind her of the poison ivy, he worried as he took the yellow floss and worked a forward knot on the left side and one backward knot on the right side.

The apartment was quiet. His mom was working and so was Manny, his stepfather. He had to hurry because they usually got home at six or so.

A key turned in the lock.

Footsteps approached, and his heart sank. His step-brother, Jayden, was blocking the doorway to their room.

"Hey, Thread Head, what are you doing now? Let me see, let me see," Jayden said, trying to wrestle the bracelet away.

"Stop, idiot!" cried Ethan, stashing the bracelet in his pants pocket.

"Pink and blue. Are you sure that's not for you?" he teased.

"Leave me alone," shouted Ethan, pushing Jayden aside.

"Or what? You'll go cry to your mama? Or maybe to your girlfriend, Olivia?" said Jayden with a laugh.

Ethan grabbed his skateboard and baseball cap. "Get a life," he muttered, slamming the front door and running down the narrow hallway.

Downstairs in front of the apartment complex, his mother was driving into the parking lot. "Ethan, it's dinnertime. Where are you going?" she called out to him.

"Nowhere," he said, pushing off in the direction of Katonah Crafts.

★ • ★ • ★

Commuters were pouring off the trains that screeched into the station every few minutes during rush hour. *Closed* said the sign in the window of the crafts store.

Propping his skateboard behind his back, Ethan plopped down on the front stoop and took out the bracelet.

When he looked up, Mr. Dalwinkle from Village Hardware was chugging full steam toward him. Only, instead of his work apron, tonight he was wearing a crisp-looking red-and-white-striped shirt and a navy-blue bow tie.

He's all duded up. Looks like he has someplace to go, Ethan thought. So he was surprised when the older gentleman stopped in front of him and was about to climb the steps up to the shop.

"It's closed," he muttered.

"What's that, son?"

"The store, Katonah Crafts, is closed," said Ethan loudly while pointing to the sign in the window.

But just then, the front door opened and Miss Ruth Ann stepped out. Ethan almost didn't recognize her.

She'd changed into a dress. Her silver-gray hair was now in soft curls, and, he couldn't believe this: *Miss Ruth Ann was wearing makeup.*

"Good evening, Philip," she said to Mr. Dalwinkle, giving him her hand. "Oh, is that you, Ethan? Did you forget something inside? I can let you in for a minute."

Ethan scrambled to his feet. "No, Miss Ruth Ann. Uh, bye," he said awkwardly and then grabbed his skateboard and pushed off, trying to cover as much distance as possible.

Rolling past Village Hardware, the crazy scene with Olivia came back—their epic fight. *Guess Olivia didn't embarrass Miss Ruth Ann after all,* he had to admit. *Who knows, maybe she even did them a favor? Yuck! TMI.*

Up ahead was a man in a khaki suit with a bouquet of flowers and a young couple holding hands and laughing. He weaved in between them and then rounded the corner up to Bedford Road. Across from the library, he hopped off. *Wow!* There was Zoe walking on the green with Carl. They looked so happy together.

She saw Ethan too and waved with a bright smile.

"Hey, Zoe," he cried. "Wait up."

He'd finish Olivia's bracelet another time or maybe give it to somebody else. He didn't think Miss Ruth Ann would throw him under the bus.

CHAPTER 37

The elevator made a pinging sound and glided to a stop on the fourth floor, where the five members of the THREADS team got out.

"The nurses' station is right up there," explained Zoe, pointing to a long wraparound desk where a dozen or so uniformed people were bustling about. "That's where we have to meet Mrs. Leon."

Olivia and Mu Mu looked around at the long corridors filled with all sorts of expensive-looking medical equipment, bulky machines, and tall, slotted food trolleys.

"Wonder what the food is like in here," whispered Mu Mu as a worker walked past carrying a tray littered with empty orange juice cartons and food wrappers. "Olivia, listen, if I'm ever stuck in a hospital, promise you'll bring me some gelato. Seriously, two kinds: toasted almond and mocha chip. Oh, and wonton soup from Golden Panda?"

Olivia laughed at that idea. "OK, you got it. Anything else?"

Across the corridor, Ethan, Austen, and Zoe were leaning against a long handrail when a woman dressed in a charcoal-gray pantsuit approached them. They straightened up and said, "Hello, Mrs. Leon."

"Hello, everybody. It's so nice to see you again," she told them. "And this must be Olivia and Mu Mu, the two poison ivy patients? All better I see." She gave them a warm smile and extended her hand.

"Nice to meet you, Mrs. Leon," said Mu Mu and Olivia.

"Well, please follow me," Mrs. Leon said, heading down another long corridor. "Ethan, Austen, and Zoe, two of our patients from last week are still here. They're looking forward to seeing you."

The door to room 412 was open. "Jacob, Nick, may we come in?" she asked, knocking. "Look who's here again: Ethan and Austen."

When the boys were settled, Mrs. Leon steered the girls down to a large, sunny lounge at the end of the hallway. It was painted in pleasant, cheerful blues and yellows, and scattered about were comfy-looking chairs and tables that were ideal for doing jigsaw puzzles or playing games.

"This is for patients and their families," Mrs. Leon explained. "Just take a seat. I'll be right back. Oh, here is Mr. Fellows, another one of our volunteers." She introduced him to everyone, and then they left.

Olivia was unpacking her supplies when Mrs. Leon returned with two young girls and a boy. They seemed so tiny and maybe a little scared.

"Their parents have gone down to the cafeteria for some coffee," Mrs. Leon explained, "so we have about half an hour, which should be plenty of time for today. Zoe, this is Noah," she said, introducing a small boy of about six, wearing a bathrobe and slippers with superheroes on them. Mr. Fellows was pulling a stand with an intravenous line and a bag of fluids behind the boy. "I thought you two could work together since you already have been here."

Zoe nodded yes and smiled at Noah.

"Perfect," said Mrs. Leon. "Then Mu Mu and Olivia, I'll go get our other two patients."

"Hi, Noah," said Zoe. "It's good to see you. Want to sit at the table with me?"

"Sure," he answered.

Olivia watched as they sat at a table by the window overlooking a small pond, and Zoe took out her flosses, scissors, and tape to attach the flosses to the table. There was also a clipboard in her backpack that would anchor the bracelet as they worked on it. Mu Mu had suggested bringing them in case the tape idea didn't work out.

"And here are Hailey and Makayla," Mrs. Leon announced, returning with two little girls about four or five. *They're way too young to be in a hospital*, thought Olivia.

"Let's all sit here, at the big table," suggested Mrs. Leon.

Like Noah, the girls were wearing bathrobes and slippers, only theirs were bright pastels and fluffy. The sleeve on Makayla's bathrobe barely concealed that her right hand was bandaged. *She can't do any work*, thought

Olivia right away. *Hope we have a bracelet she likes that we can give her.*

"Makayla, want to sit next to me?" Mu Mu said, pulling out a chair.

"I fell from the swing," said Makayla, showing her arm to Mu Mu.

"I'm sorry," said Mu Mu. "Bet that hurt!"

Makayla nodded.

Mrs. Leon patted the seat of the chair next to her. "And, Hailey, you sit here in between Olivia and me," she suggested. "Now, children, people have been making friendship bracelets for a long, long time. But, Olivia, why don't you tell the girls more about them? For instance, I see you are wearing some. Are there stories behind them?"

"Yes, there are stories for each one," she said, pointing to them. "Let me start with this one with our name on it, THREADS. Do you both know what a club is?"

★ • ★ • ★

Later at Katonah Crafts, Olivia was opening one of the drawers in the floss cabinet. "That was so awesome!" she laughed. "Anybody else need more blue?"

"I do," said Ethan. "Bright electric blue, cobalt blue, and sapphire."

"Anything else?" asked Olivia, handing them over.

Mu Mu looked up. "I could use some powder blue. And what's that pinky-white floss called?"

"Seashell," both Ethan and Olivia replied.

"Yup, that's it," Mu Mu said, reaching out. "You know Hailey is only five, but she was good at making a simple braid. She really liked your blue-and-white braid, Olivia. I'll make her one and bring it next week."

"And Noah caught on fast too," said Zoe. "He started on a braid in purple, blue, pale green, and black. He's going home on Friday, so I left it with him," she told Ethan and Austen. "How did you guys do with Jacob and Nick?"

Ethan and Austen glanced at each other. Austen raised his hand in a "you go first" gesture.

"They already finished the bracelets from last week: the arrow, in mustard yellow, viridian blue, raspberry, and lime green," said Ethan.

"So today we started them with the chevron pattern,"

Austen continued. "And they're both going home maybe this week, so we showed them how to finish the bracelets by themselves, right, buddy?"

Ethan nodded.

"Cool!" the girls said together. Ethan and Austen gave each other a high five.

Miss Ruth Ann looked over from behind the counter and smiled. The doorbell rang, and the mail carrier sprinted in with a package.

"Oh, look, it's from Floss World," Miss Ruth Ann said, opening the box. "Must be the new colors, Ethan."

"Cool," he said.

Mu Mu, Zoe, Austen, and Olivia all looked at each other and rolled their eyes. Ethan caught them.

"OK, OK," he said with a laugh. "So I'm a thread head."

"Then so are we," laughed Zoe, and the other members of THREADS joined in.

CHAPTER 38

Camp was quiet.

The skies were overcast, turning dark and inky. The director couldn't decide whether or not to dismiss the campers for the day, so everyone was staying close to home base by the picnic tables until she made the call.

"Looks like it's going to pour, if you ask me," Mu Mu said to Olivia while pointing at the sky. "Can I come to your house if it rains? Mom is at an open house. One of the agents at Lin Realty called in sick."

"Oh, sure," Olivia replied, looking up. "And Zoe said she was going to be home all day. Maybe she can come over too."

"Super!" said Mu Mu.

"And guess what! My mom bought some fancy

chocolate chips yesterday. Maybe we could make one of your recipes?"

"Ooh." Mu Mu smiled. "Now I'm going to actually pray for rain!"

Olivia gave her a fist bump. But then the smile on Mu Mu's face disappeared like the sun behind those rain clouds.

"Look at six o'clock," she muttered, pointing over Olivia's shoulder.

Olivia swiveled and glanced at the camp entrance. Elin Pierson and Kennedy Washington were strolling in, and unfortunately, they seemed to be heading right toward them. Olivia's body tensed up, and she thought, *This must be what it's like to see a tornado approaching. Well, maybe that's too much. Maybe a squall?*

"Stand your ground," whispered Mu Mu. "Don't even look their way!"

Meanwhile, Ashley and Parker also caught sight of the two former campers and hurried over to them. Olivia and Mu Mu watched as they spoke for a few minutes. Ashley was gesturing with a "you listen to me" attitude.

Erin and Kennedy nodded their heads up and down, and then all four walked over to the picnic table.

"OK, listen up. All eleven/twelve girls, please form a circle here," Ashley said, pointing to a spot right in front of her. Olivia noticed that Parker, who had moved to the side, was taking out her phone. *This is a funny time to make a call*, she thought.

Ashley continued, "As you all are aware, Team Unicorn has been down two members since the recent unfortunate incident in Carey's Woods. Elin Pierson and Kennedy Washington have something they would like to say to you now."

Mu Mu nudged Olivia and gestured toward Parker. She was recording everything.

With a shake of her head, Elin flicked her long, blond hair over her shoulder and said in a quiet voice, "We're both very sorry for what happened."

Kennedy nodded as Elin spoke.

"And we're sorry if anyone got poison ivy," Elin continued.

The campers stood there silently.

"OK, everybody, let's put this behind us," said Ashley. "I'm sure Elin and Kennedy are sincere in their apology. Let's give them a big hurrah for being so brave."

A few campers shouted, "Yay!" But Mu Mu and Olivia were not among them.

Elin smiled and looked like she was about to leave, but then she stopped and said to the group, "Just so you know, honestly, it wasn't our fault. We thought Olivia and Mu Mu were stepping back into us and we put up our hands to stop them. After all, I *was* wearing my new sneakers."

"Yes, she was!" cried Kennedy, pointing to Elin's feet. Olivia gasped.

"Oh please!" shouted Mu Mu. "That will so not fly!"

The first of the raindrops started falling.

"Camp dismissed!" cried Ashley.

★ • ★ • ★

Zoe shook her head. "I can't believe it!" she said. "Wow! And I especially can't believe your counselor bought that lame story. Not in a trillion years would my mom have swallowed that!"

The rain was pelting against the windows in Zoe's bedroom, or Alex's old room, as Olivia still thought of it. She remembered the time a branch flew against it and broke one of the panes. Even today, she could remember which one was repaired.

"Yup, Elin is outrageous," added Mu Mu.

"She's trouble," said Zoe.

"Double trouble," Mu Mu said. "Oh, and speaking of double, we made double-chocolate-chip cookies at Olivia's. We left a big bag downstairs on your kitchen counter. Are you hungry?"

"For chocolate-chip cookies? Always!" said Zoe, scooping up Carl and heading down to the kitchen.

A weird, sad feeling washed over Olivia. She didn't feel good about anything. Before she could stop herself, she invented an excuse and blurted out, "You know what? I've got to go over to Katonah Crafts. I forgot all about promising to help out Miss Ruth Ann."

"Right now? Don't you want to try the cookies?" asked Mu Mu, a little surprised.

"Oh, yeah, sure I do. Save me some?" she said.

"Mu Mu, I can text you if you want to come back to my house."

"Oh, stay here, Mu Mu," Zoe urged. "You can help me with Carl. I'm trying to teach him to sit."

Carl looked up at them and then ran to the back door.

"Look, he's so smart. He needs to go out!" said Mu Mu. "He's teaching us!"

Main Street was quiet. Even though it was raining lightly, Olivia walked slowly. She didn't have to go to Katonah Crafts. Seriously, she needed to be alone for a while. The gazebo was empty, so she headed there and plopped down on the bench.

I don't know why I feel so bad, she thought, while nervously twisting her mom's blue-and-white friendship bracelet. *It isn't just the Elin and Kennedy thing. What's bothering me is Alex. I still miss her like crazy. My new friends are nice, but what about old friends? Is that what life is, getting close to people and then losing them?*

She remembered a saying Alex's mother had on a pillow: *Make new friends but keep the old. One is silver, the other gold.* A train was pulling out of the station on its way to New York City. *Just like Alex had to pull away from me*, she thought, pleased with the imagery.

But then she realized, *Maybe in time, my new friends will become gold? Oh, it's just too much. I can't even deal with this!*

"Hey, beautiful, what are you doing here?" someone said, breaking in on her questions about life.

She swung around. It was Jayden, Ethan's stepbrother.

"Oh, nothing," she answered, on guard.

"So how come Thread Head isn't with you? Thought you two were knotted together. Seriously, what are you wasting your time with a nerd like him for anyway? Why don't you let me buy you a soda?" he asked with a smirk.

Olivia almost laughed, thinking, *Double trouble, wasn't that what Mu Mu and Zoe said about Elin? Well, they should check out this guy.*

Then, as if the fates were sending her a great big special delivery gift, the door to Katonah Cupcakes opened. Out walked Elin Pierson—that's right, Elin Pierson—in her most-dazzling princess hairstyle ever, with long, long curls and a pearl crown. Something drew her eyes across the street, and she stopped dead in her tracks when she saw Olivia with Jayden.

"Hi, Elin," Olivia shouted with a wave.

Elin sauntered toward them and as she did, she brought her A game: her walk got more and more stuck-up and her entire attitude more princessy, practically royal. She even put on her sunglasses. In the rain! Talk about throwing shade!

"Oh, Elin," called out Olivia, jumping up. "Have you met Jayden yet?"

Like a miracle, Elin went for the bait, crossed the street, and then, Olivia reeled her in. "This is Jayden," said Olivia. "He helps Mr. Dalwinkle at Village Hardware." Nobody said anything, so she slipped away, practically doing a jig. "Sorry, I've got to go. Bye, bye," she said in a high voice with a wave.

When Olivia was across the street, she turned around. She was planning to put on a super pathetic face in case they were watching, but she didn't have to. Elin was already sitting next to Jayden. He was taking her photo… Oh, and now they were exchanging phone numbers.

Yes! It was such a great moment for her. Olivia could almost hear "Nessun Dorma" playing and the sound of cymbals crashing: "*Vincero! Vincero! Vincero!*"

CHAPTER 39

Maybe I will help Miss Ruth Ann, Olivia thought and hurried down Main Street.

"Oh, hi, Ethan. Just saw your stepbrother, Jayden, in town," she said, entering Katonah Crafts.

"That's cool," muttered Ethan, absorbed in the new flosses, yarns, and cords catalog.

Olivia shrugged and walked over to the counter. "Hi, Miss Ruth Ann," she said with a smile. "You look very nice today. I like your dress."

Miss Ruth Ann smiled back and patted her hair. "Thank you, dear," she said.

With a jerk of his head, Ethan looked over, and then he gave Miss Ruth Ann a thumbs-up.

Both Olivia and Miss Ruth Ann started to laugh.

"What's so funny?" said Olivia's mom, opening the front door. "Oh, that rain. I'm soaked! It just started coming down hard."

Olivia hurried over to help her mom with her umbrella. "Is there anything I can do here today?" Olivia asked, looking around.

Miss Ruth Ann pointed to an unopened carton. "Well, we need the new flosses put away in the floss cabinet," she said, opening a drawer. "You know how we like to line them up like so."

Olivia nodded. Ever since she was really little, that had been one of her favorite jobs.

After thirty minutes or so, the skeins of floss were perfect.

"Anything else?" she asked.

"Let's see, we put away the flosses, organized the bead bins, set up the new coloring book section. I'd say we're good," answered her mom. "But, sweetie, where is Mu Mu? Weren't you spending the afternoon with her?"

Yipes! Mu Mu. Olivia had forgotten all about her.

"She's at Zoe's. I'm going there now," she said quickly. "Her mom is picking her up soon."

"I'll go with you," piped up Ethan, getting out of his chair and stretching. "Looks like the rain stopped."

When they knocked, Zoe opened the door with puppy Carl in her arms. "Hey, hi, come on in, guys," she said. "You know, Ethan, I was going to text you. I need some help with this bracelet I'm working on." She led him off to the screened-in porch.

In the kitchen, Mu Mu was sitting at the long island.

"So, how were the cookies?" Olivia asked, looking at an empty plastic bag.

"They were great. Zoe's dad ate most of them. But I have to get back to your house. My mom is picking me up in a while."

Olivia nodded, and after saying good-bye to Zoe and Ethan, they scooted out. Raindrops were still falling from the trees on Bedford Road, so they dashed across the green and headed up to Olivia's front porch, where it was dry and cozy.

"Mom should be here in a couple of minutes, so can

we wait outside?" asked Mu Mu, pointing to the round table.

"Oh, sure, but let me get Sullivan," she said, opening the front door. The big dog bounded out of the house and immediately covered Mu Mu with kisses.

"It's hard to believe this is how big Carl will get," she laughed, trying to get some air.

"Oh, Carl will be even bigger!" said Olivia, pulling him off Mu Mu and trying to control him. "That's right, Sully, we're talking about Carl, your big baby brother. Now sit."

Mu Mu laughed. "But you know what, Olivia? Zoe's father really loved the chocolate-chip cookies. And he writes a food blog. Did you know that? Isn't that the coolest thing?"

"Yep. Very cool," agreed Olivia.

"So I told him about my chocolate-chip cookie quest, and he asked me to write a little bit about it. It could be fun!" she said. "He already told me how much they like Golden Panda—oh, there's Mom. TTYL!"

Her mother pulled up, and Mu Mu waved good-bye.

Wow! That could be really cool for her, thought Olivia, realizing that even though Mu Mu talked about food a lot, she didn't seem to overeat, and she was so tiny! Maybe there was such a thing as a food prodigy? Like a piano prodigy or a violin prodigy? Or flute—which reminded her how she had been neglecting her flute since she got braces.

"Let's go, Sully," she said, heading upstairs. She was opening the flute case when it came to her: *Wait a minute. Mu Mu is just as good at making friendship bracelets as Ethan. Yet Zoe asked him for help. Oh, wow! That's interesting.*

CHAPTER 40

The community garden was down Pawley Road, a dirt road that wound past big horse farms. Olivia loved the look of the pristine, white fences that enclosed the meadows. Every now and then, she could see an actual horse or two frolicking in the sun.

They passed the old train station, and Olivia kept an eye out for the large area with the eight-foot-high fence Austen had told her about.

"That's to keep out the deer," he had explained. "They're all over the place up here."

Even in a much busier place like the village, Olivia had seen deer too, near her house, but her mom wouldn't put up a fence. She kept saying that Sully would keep them at bay.

Yesterday, Austen texted Olivia to come over at two o'clock. It was a good time for him, before the sun got overly hot, and when a lot of people had already gone home for the day.

It was a good time for her too, after camp when she could change into her new lacy white top and aqua shorts.

"Austen said to park anywhere," Olivia explained to her mom. "Look, there's a good spot, next to the big gate."

They walked in and saw a grid of beautifully tended raised beds. "Keep an eye out for asparagus," said her mom, leaning over. "That's what I want to plant in the backyard."

A few of the gardeners smiled as they passed.

"Oh, look," said Olivia's mom, pointing to a figure a few rows over. "It's Mrs. Vreeland, from the library. You know her. She's such a sweet person. She comes into Katonah Crafts all the time for yarn too."

"Sure, for her needlepoint," recalled Olivia.

"Angela, hello," called her mom, waving to her.

Mrs. Vreeland straightened up and waved back.

Before Olivia's mom could scoot away, Austen walked by pushing a wheelbarrow full of compost.

"Hi, Mrs. Jones. Hi, Olivia," he said, putting it down. "Sorry this is so stinky."

"Yipes!" cried Olivia wrinkling her nose. "It's stinky all right."

A moment later, Mrs. Vreeland joined them. "Well, how are you all?" she said. "Olivia, you have grown so much! You look wonderful! Now, I see you are chatting with my grandson Austen. Do you know Mrs. Jones and her daughter, Olivia, Austen dear?"

Austen nodded. "Yes, Nana," he said with a smile.

"Oh, Austen is your grandson, Angela?" said Olivia's mom right away. "Well, let me tell you how wonderful he is! My husband just adores him! But didn't I see you standing by an asparagus bed? That's what I want to plant."

The two ladies walked away, chatting happily.

Austen and Olivia looked at each other. "Well, I'm glad your father adores me," said Austen with a laugh. "That's a good start."

Olivia laughed too. "What are you doing with that?" she asked, pointing to the wheelbarrow.

"People come by and drop off their extra compost,

and now I'm adding it to our big pile. Would you like to see it?"

"Love to!" said Olivia.

Austen smiled. "And, if you play your cards right, I might even let you aerate the compost. We have to do that so all the debris will turn into humus."

The compost was separated in a big area that was some distance from the main part of the garden. As they passed some of the raised gardens, Austen pointed out the different vegetables and flowers that were shooting up.

Olivia was amazed by what he knew. "Are there any daisies here? That's my favorite flower," she said.

"Which ones? The white, like, Shasta daisies?"

Olivia nodded.

"I'll keep that in mind," he said. "We have a big, big garden at home. Mom and Dad always make us work in it, but it's fun."

"My mom has a garden too, but it's nothing like this," she said, looking across at her mother chatting away with Mrs. Vreeland. "Hope your grandmother isn't giving her too many ideas," she said, thinking of how much work it is to turn the soil and put in new beds.

As if he read her mind, Austen said, "Be careful. Nana is great at inspiring people."

Olivia gave him a big smile and didn't even think about her blue-and-white braces.

"It's cool that Mrs. Vreeland is your grandmother. I think I've known her all my life," she said just as they got to the compost pile, and Austen set down the wheelbarrow.

Boy, I would hate to fall into this, Olivia thought, staring at the moldering heap and taking a few steps away from it. *Poison ivy was bad enough, but at least it didn't stink!*

She turned to see Austen gazing at her.

"Olivia," he said almost in a whisper, "don't laugh, but I made something for you, and I wanted to give it to you before I get all grungy with this compost." He reached into a pocket in his cargo shorts.

Olivia looked down. He was holding out a friendship bracelet in purple with *OLLIE* spelled out in pink.

"Ooh," she gasped. "You made this? It's absolutely amazing!"

"Your color chart says purple is for beautiful and pink for sweet, so I thought that was you. But there are lots of mistakes," said Austen, tying it on for her.

"You know what, Austen? You're definitely not a mistake," she said, twirling it with a laugh. *I don't care how much stinky compost he has to shovel. I'll wait until he's done,* she thought.

CHAPTER 41

"Alex, it's so beautiful I can't keep my eyes off it," said Olivia, caressing her new friendship bracelet. "I'm taking it to Nantucket."

Camp would be over at the end of the week, and the girls were catching up on their vacation plans. It was a tender topic because this would be the first summer since forever that Alex had not been with them.

"Dad is making us leave first thing Saturday morning as usual, so maybe you and I can Skype on Sunday? Oh, I'll send you a pic of the ferry," said Olivia.

"Sure thing. But what about THREADS?" asked Alex. "Will someone cover for you?"

Olivia laughed. "Of course. Ethan has worked that

all out! But really, Alex, Ethan is actually becoming a human being. The kids in the hospital are so great."

Alex wasn't fooled by Olivia's cheerful tone. She knew Nantucket would be lonely for her friend. "Send me pics of the Juice Bar and Jetties Beach and any new T-shirt shops that have opened," she said. "And watch out for the seagulls at the ferry! Love you!"

CHAPTER 42

"Come on, Ollie. You've got to get everything packed tonight," Olivia's dad was saying. "You know we have to leave at five in the morning in order to catch the noon ferry."

It was the eve of the Joneses' annual family vacation in Nantucket. For one amazing whole week, they would live in a beach cottage, swim all day long, and fall asleep to the sound of the surf.

As Olivia took out her big floral tote, she remembered the summer Alex had been losing her first tooth and Olivia's mom had taken them over to the Cottage Hospital. A sweet, young doctor gave the tooth a good yank, and out it came. Then, he gave Alex a small plastic box shaped like a treasure chest to put it in. The girls couldn't believe the tooth fairy found them all the way in Nantucket, and for years afterward, that's where Olivia thought all fairies lived.

There was the time they set up a lemonade stand in the front yard. After about three hours, they'd made four dollars, and then they had so much fun spending it in the tiny Corner Market that always had lots of fresh dough-nuts and cookies.

"We'll have a great time," Olivia's mom kept saying over and over. "You know how we love the shops and walking down the cobblestone streets to see all the houses."

She's right, thought Olivia, packing up her new bath-ing suit and flip-flops. *There is a ton of stuff to do there. Dad said we could go out on a whale watch. Mom wants to go on the garden tour. That's cool too. I wonder if I can eat lobster with my braces.*

"OK, Sully, we're finished," she said, turning out the light and snuggling under her summer quilt, which she had to remember to bring with her tomorrow.

"Go to sleep now. We have to get up super early," she told him.

The five-hour ride up was easy. Sully slept most of the way north up Route 95. Olivia texted Mu Mu and Zoe, and she promised Mu Mu lots of chocolate-covered cranberries and Zoe some homemade dog biscuits from Cold Noses, her favorite pet shop, down the street from the harbor.

As they neared Hyannis on the mainland, where they'd catch the ferry, Olivia's phone chimed. It was a new pic from Austen. She actually laughed out loud. He had taken it in front of the compost pile and was holding his fingers in the shape of a heart. That was so romantic!

She started to wonder, *What can I get him? It can't be anything touristy… I know, the most beautiful seashells I can find. That will keep me busy.*

The ferry ride over would be long—two and a half hours long—so she was extra glad she had packed her flosses. Maybe she would try making a bracelet with a whale. Ethan had given her the pattern before she'd left. Plus, he'd promised to help Miss Ruth Ann in the store while they were away. Zoe said she would stop in and help too. *Hmm…that was nice of her*, Olivia thought.

In the crowded lot at the Steamship Authority, lines and lines of SUVs, trucks, and cars waited their turn to board the gaping mouth on the big ferry. A burly seaman pointed to where her dad should park his ancient Land Cruiser and wait for their turn. They were more than an hour early, as usual, but the good news was they could get out of their car and stretch their legs.

Olivia started to reach for her backpack when she noticed the blue-and-white friendship bracelet, the special one from Dawn. It was looking extra frayed. "Mom, the bracelet you gave me is almost falling apart. Do you have a safety pin?" Olivia asked, worried she would lose it again.

"I think so, sweetie, but let me get out the ferry reservations first," she said, going through her overcrowded tote bag.

Her dad put out his palm.

"Yes, honey, I'm looking for them," Olivia's mom said. "I know they're in here."

Olivia sighed. They went through the same thing every year. Her mom's inability to find the reservations was as much a part of the vacation ritual as their fast-food stops on the long drive up or ice cream cones at the Nantucket Juice Bar once they arrived.

Finally, the paperwork was straightened out, and the three straggled inside the main terminal overlooking the harbor. Sullivan loved the ferry and was happy to see other dogs waiting to get onboard. He was still young and wild, so her dad kept him on a tight leash.

"Don't let him jump on me," said Olivia. "I don't want this bracelet to fall off. It's on life support as it is."

"You know, sweetie, a friendship bracelet is supposed to fall off when your wish comes true," her mom said.

"I know, I know, but it hasn't yet, so do you have that safety pin?" Olivia answered, looking at her wrist.

She didn't want to tell her parents that her wish was that Alex could have come with them. That would make them think she wasn't happy or that she was disappointed in some way with the vacation.

"Oh, Ollie, I think I know what your wish is," said her mom.

"Really?"

"Uh-huh."

She pointed to the electric eye doors at the main entrance. They went *whoosh* and a small group of people walked in. At the rear, Olivia could see a very tall man—a very tall man with his arm around the neck of a dark-haired, young girl.

"OMG! Alex! Alex!" screamed Olivia, "OMG, Mom. It's Alex!" She streaked across the floor and flung herself into the arms of her BFF.

Olivia's dad let go of Sullivan's leash, and Sullivan bounded over to Alex too, wagging his tail wildly and jumping all over them.

"Don't worry. I'm getting it," Olivia's mom told her dad while videoing the reunion with her phone. Alex's father waved to them. Before Olivia's mom could stop him, Alex's father leaned over and picked up something from the floor. He flung it outside, and right away, a seagull swooped down and, in one graceful arc, nabbed it with its long bill and then sailed up toward the sky.

Olivia's mom kept recording as Dawn's blue-and-white

friendship bracelet soared higher and higher over Nantucket Bay until it was completely out of sight. She knew Olivia would appreciate the poetry in that.

HOW TO MAKE YOUR OWN FRIENDSHIP BRACELET

Weave it!

You will need embroidery thread in four colors (this makes it easy if you're a beginner!). Cut one yard of each color so that you have four strings. Arrange the strings by color in the way that you want them to show on your bracelet.

1. Tie all the strings together with a regular knot, and leave about a 2-inch tail above the knot. You can tape the tail to a table, pin it to your jeans, or find another way to keep it in place.

2. Starting with string A (on the left), wrap it over and then under string B. This will make a knot.

3. Make sure you make it tight. Pull string A up while you hold down string B.

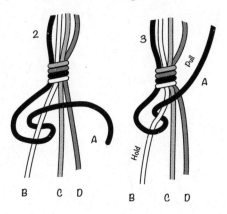

4. Using string A over string B again, make another knot like in step 2. Tighten it up the same way.

5. Now you're done with string B! Next, take string A and make 2 knots on string C (just like you did on string B). Repeat again on string D. When you're done, string A will be all the way on the right. Congrats! You just finished your first row!

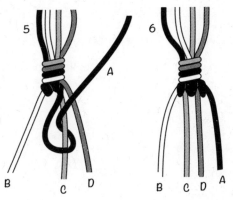

6. Start the next row by using string B (which is now the first on the left) to make 2 knots each on string C, D, and then A. Always start a new row from the left.

7. Repeat to make more rows until your bracelet is long enough to wear.

Wear it!

When you're done, make another knot at the end with all the strings to keep it together. Before you cut off any extra string, tie it on your wrist or ankle. The best way to keep it in place is with a square knot (first you tie it right over left, and then the second knot left over right). Now you can cut the strings. Make sure you leave around an inch of string for the tails.

ACKNOWLEDGMENTS

To Steve Geck, my editor at Sourcebooks, I am deeply grateful for his inspired idea of spinning a story around friendship bracelets. I would also like to thank Josalyn Moran and my agent Patricia Brigandi plus my extremely patient sister Mo Stewart.

LOOK OUT FOR THE NEXT BOOK IN
THE FRIENDSHIP BRACELET SERIES!

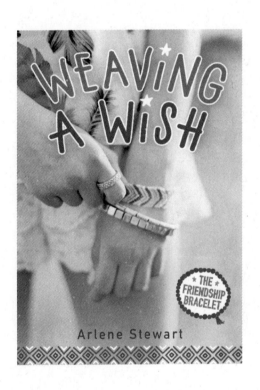

ABOUT THE AUTHOR

In *The Friendship Bracelet*, Arlene Stewart weaves together her love of crafts with her fond memories of Katonah, New York, where she raised her daughter Annalee. The author of several crafts books, she also created the long-running "Teen Quiz" series with Annalee and her BFF Jana Peterson.